A Friend for Caitlin

written by Lynea Bowdish

illustrated by Meredith Johnson

For Vicki—who, like Ralph,
has always been there

First printing by Willowisp Press 1998.

Published by PAGES Publishing Group
801 94th Avenue North, St. Petersburg, Florida 33702

Printed in the United States of America

Willowisp Press®

2 4 6 8 10 9 7 5 3 1

ISBN 0-87406-894-0

Chapter One

"There she is!" I whispered. I ducked behind the kitchen curtain so the girl next door wouldn't see me.

"Caitlin, why don't you just go out and say hello?" my mother asked.

"By myself?" I said. "No way."

Mom worked on her laptop computer at the kitchen. She knew I wasn't good at meeting new people, but she kept trying to help me get over it.

I peeked around the curtain.

"She has long, dark brown hair, just like Krista's," I said. "And a big dog like Sparky."

3

Sparky was Krista's dog. Krista and I had been friends forever. She and her family had moved to California last month.

I watched the girl hook the dog's chain to the front of Sparky's doghouse. Then she kissed her dog on the nose and went into Krista's old house.

"Just like Krista," I said. "Krista always kissed Sparky on the nose."

The new girl looked like Krista, had a dog like Krista, and lived in Krista's house. It was perfect. I just knew we were meant to be friends. But how was I ever going to meet her?

"Well," Mom said, "if you're not going over there this morning, you'll have to find something to do here. I still have some work to finish."

"I could make another batch of brownies," I answered. I was always trying to invent a new kind. I used a box mix and then added

other things. I hadn't come up with anything great yet, but I kept trying. I took out a bowl to make some brownies. This time I decided to add a can of pineapple.

"We have to become friends before school starts," I told Mom. "I can't walk to school by myself."

"You can walk to school with Ralph," Mom said.

"Ralph's a whole year younger than I am, and he's a whole grade behind me. Besides, he's a boy," I answered.

It's not that I didn't like Ralph. I did. He never called me "Cait." And he was always doing something new. Lately, he was trying to learn to stand on his head.

"Caitlin, I know you miss Krista," Mom said, "but you'll make a lot of new friends at school this year."

"I'm no good at making friends," I said.

"Krista was my friend since before I can remember. She just happened."

Krista and I had done everything together. We both loved science fiction movies, and we collected posters of rock groups. Best of all, we kept looking for new ways to fix ponytails. We were up to eleven when she moved.

Of course, I liked doing some things by myself. I read mysteries and stories about horses. But other things were more fun to do with someone. And some things were just easier with a friend. Like walking to school on the first day. And meeting a bunch of new people.

I stirred the brownie batter one more time. Then I heard the back door open. I wiped my hands on a towel and looked over to see who was there.

Ralph stuck his head in. He didn't knock. He never does.

"Great news!" Ralph said. "The new girl's name is Briney Manelli, and she's your age."

It *was* great news. Almost as good as having Krista back. If only I could figure out how to meet her.

Chapter Two

"How do you know the new girl's name?" I asked Ralph.

"The movers told me," he said. Ralph can find out anything about anybody.

I spooned the brownie mix into the pan.

"What kind of brownies are you making this time?" Ralph asked.

"Pineapple," I said as Mom put them in the oven for me.

"P-A," Ralph said, making a face. Ralph talks in initials.

"Perfectly Awesome?" I asked.

"Pretty Awful," he said.

We went outside to wait for the brownies to bake. Ralph rolled over onto his head. He can't go long without trying to stand on his head. He told me he wants to do it while he's short. He figured it will be harder when he gets taller. His hands were always dirty from trying. This time Ralph got his knees into the air before he fell onto the grass.

"How can I meet her?" I asked.

"Just go over and say 'hi,'" Ralph said.

"You sound like my mother," I said. "I'm not good at making friends. You're the one who makes friends with everyone."

It was true. Ralph had lots of friends because he was so easy to talk to.

I stared at the ground. If Briney Manelli became my friend, we could walk to school together. And collect posters. And try eleven different ways to do ponytails. Just like Krista and I. If only I could make friends like Ralph.

Then I got an idea. But I had to figure out how to get Ralph to say "yes" to it. And I knew just the thing to make him agree.

Ralph collected things, like the stickers on bananas. So far he had found eight different ones. He also collected posters of rock stars, like Krista and I did.

"Ralph, you know that poster of mine you like—the one of the Oxy-Morons?" I asked.

"It's an S-P," he said.

I thought a moment. "A Special Poster?" I asked.

He shook his head and said, "A Super Pin-up."

"Would you like to have it?" I asked.

"Are you kidding? What do I have to do?"

"You have to help me with something," I said. "I'll even throw in some brownies."

Ralph loved brownies as much as he loved posters.

"Help you with what?" Ralph asked.

I grinned. "You're going to teach me how to make friends with Briney Manelli."

Chapter Three

Ralph and I agreed that I had to meet Briney. But that was the *only* thing we agreed on.

"Why do I have to go with you?" Ralph asked.

"Because I don't know what to say," I said. "If you don't come with me, I'm not going. Then you don't get the poster. Or the brownies. And remember, you have to do all the talking."

Ralph knew I was stubborn. So he gave in.

"Those brownies had better not have pineapple in them," he grumbled. "I want N-A."

"Nuts and Applesauce?" I asked.

"Nothing Added," he said.

The walk next door seemed endless. When Krista lived there, it was so close.

I stopped when I reached Briney's sidewalk. The house didn't look friendly. Not like when Krista was there. The dog barked from the backyard.

Ralph gave me a little push.

"Let's go," he said.

I stood behind him at the door. My mouth was dry. My stomach shook like it always did when I had to meet strangers.

"You can't even ring the bell?" Ralph asked me.

I shook my head. My mouth wouldn't work.

Ralph pushed the doorbell button and we waited. And waited. Of course, Ralph couldn't just wait. He had to try standing on his head. He had just fallen into the bush by the steps when the door opened.

I couldn't help staring at Briney. I hadn't seen anyone so pretty since Krista.

Ralph jumped to his feet and stuck out a dirty hand. "Are you Briney Manelli?" Ralph asked with a big smile.

The girl stared at his hand without taking it and nodded.

"My name is Ralph McKenny. This is Caitlin Collier." Ralph's smile got even bigger. "We want to welcome you to the neighborhood."

The girl didn't say anything. She looked at Ralph from the top of his head to the toes of his shoes and then back up again. I couldn't help looking, too. Ralph's stiff, blond hair stood straight up. His glasses slid down his nose. His bony legs stuck out of his shorts. My dad said Ralph looks like an upside-down broom. My mom said he'll outgrow it.

Then Briney looked at me.

My hair is mud brown, not dark chocolate brown like Briney's and Krista's. My eighth

way to do a ponytail was already starting to
fall down. And I couldn't think of anything to
say. Briney looked back at Ralph.

"Thank you," she said.

She didn't sound as if she meant it.

"We're unpacking," Briney said. "I have to
go now."

With that, Briney Manelli closed the door.

Chapter

Four

"She was busy," I told Ralph when we got back to his house. I knew I was making excuses, but Krista had never done anything like that.

"She was T-R," Ralph said.

"Terribly Rushed?" I asked.

"Totally Rude," Ralph said.

"She sure is pretty, though," I said. "She'll make all the friends she wants when school starts." We sat down on the living room floor.

"Not if she's always that rude," Ralph said. Then he mumbled, "Maybe this isn't a good idea."

I thought about Krista. She always had time for me.

"Caitlin Collier never gives up," I said.
"We just need another plan."

"I have to think," Ralph said.

He rolled over onto his head. His mother
let him try standing on his head anywhere.
She said the house was Ralph-proofed. Dad
said that means Ralph has already broken
everything that's breakable. Mom said it means
his mother has moved things.

Ralph's feet crashed against the coffee table
and a pile of magazines slid to the floor.

"I've got it!" Ralph said. "Ask her to come over to your house tomorrow. You can get to know each other."

I felt tongue-tied just thinking about it. I never had trouble talking to Krista or Ralph. Of course, Krista and Ralph had never shut the door in my face.

"What will we talk about?" I asked.

"Show her your posters," Ralph said. "Talk about them."

"How do I ask her over?" I asked.

"Call her up," Ralph said.

"No!" I almost yelled the word. "I can't. Besides, I don't know her number."

"Then stick a note in her mailbox," Ralph said.

What if she saw me? What if she came out and I had to explain what I was doing?

"Will you put it in her mailbox for me?" I asked.

Ralph sighed. "Anything for the Oxy-Morons," he said.

We wrote the note together.

Dear Briney,
 You are invited to my house
 on Thursday afternoon at
 three o'clock. Please come.
                        Sincerely,
                        Caitlin

I wrote my address under my name.

"Make sure you're at my house *before* three o'clock," I told Ralph.

"Why?" Ralph asked.

"Because I don't want to be alone with her yet," I said. "You have to come or I won't do it."

"Okay," Ralph said. "But only because I want to see if she's always rude."

"She won't be," I said. "We're going to be good friends."

I just hoped I was right.

Chapter Five

On Thursday Ralph showed up before Briney, but I was still nervous. Then Briney came—at exactly three o'clock.

"My mother says people shouldn't be late," Briney said as she walked in.

Ralph looked at me.

"Would you like to see my ponytail pictures?" I asked Briney.

She shrugged.

I took out my scrapbook. I opened it to a picture of a ponytail that had been braided with ribbons.

"This is my favorite one," I said, showing Briney. "Maybe we can try it."

Briney tossed her long hair behind her shoulder. "I never wear a ponytail," she said. "My mother says it's bad for my hair."

Her mother sure had a lot of rules.

"I'll show you my posters," I said.

Ralph trailed along behind us to my room. The walls were covered with posters, like Krista's room had been.

As soon as we stepped into the room, Ralph rolled onto his head.

"What's he doing?" Briney asked.

"Trying to stand on his head," I said.

"It's T-F," Ralph said.

"Terribly Foolish?" I asked.

"Totally Fun," he said, falling over. Ralph's feet crashed into the bed.

I slipped an Oxy-Morons CD into the CD player.

As soon as the music began, Ralph started dancing around the room. I couldn't help tapping my foot. If Krista had been in the room, we'd both be dancing along with Ralph. Briney just listened.

Halfway through the first song, she said, "Don't you have any jazz? I don't like rock. It's boring."

Ralph stopped dancing and stared at Briney. I stopped the CD before he could say anything and picked out another one.

"Maybe you'll like this one better," I said.

"Never mind," Briney said. "I've got to go anyway."

Without saying another word, Briney Manelli turned around and left.

When we heard the front door shut, Ralph and I looked at each other and shrugged.

"Maybe I'll have to walk to school by myself," I said.

"It might be better than walking with her," Ralph said. "She's rude and mean and *very*

unfriendly."

"I guess this wasn't such a good idea," I said.

I must have sounded sad or something, because Ralph patted me on the shoulder.

"You never give up," he said. "Think of it like your brownies. There's always something else to try."

I laughed. Ralph was good at cheering me up. And he was right. Whenever the brownies tasted awful, I just tried something else.

"How about the movies?" he asked. "Everyone likes the movies. And you won't have to talk much. Think you can try inviting her this time?"

I nodded.

"But only if you go with us," I said.

Ralph agreed. I knew he would. Ralph loved the movies.

I really, really hoped that Briney did, too.

Chapter Six

"That was a dumb movie," Briney said when we came out of the movies the next day. "I don't know why my mother made me go with you two."

"I thought it was one of the best sci-fi movies I've ever seen," Ralph said. "S-S-F."

"Simply Super Film?" I asked.

"Special Sci-Fi," Ralph said.

Briney flipped her hair over her shoulder. "The special effects were stupid," she said.

I didn't look at Ralph. I thought the movie was great. But somehow I didn't feel so good about it anymore.

At her house, Briney turned away without

saying good-bye and walked right up to her front door.

"Next time we'll skip science fiction," I called after her.

"Next time *I'll* pick the movie," Briney said. And she closed the door behind her.

Ralph and I walked toward my house in silence.

"Not everyone likes every movie," I said when we got to my sidewalk.

"Briney thinks anyone who likes this one is a jerk," Ralph said.

I didn't say anything. Something inside me agreed with him. Krista would have loved the movie.

"We should give up," Ralph said.

Part of me wanted to, but then I thought about walking to school by myself. And I thought about Krista.

"Let's try once more," I said. "Just one

more time."

Ralph sighed. "Okay," he said. "But it's time for a new idea."

He rolled over onto his head on the front

lawn. This time he got his feet in the air before he fell over. We sat down on the front steps.

"Krista and I liked the same things," I said. "But Briney doesn't like anything I like."

"We've got to find something you two can do together," Ralph said. He sat up. "I know! We'll find out what *she* likes."

"How do we do that?" I asked.

"We have to get you inside Briney's house. Then you can see what she likes to do," he answered.

Ralph and I sat and thought some more. Then I got a delicious idea.

"I'll bring her some brownies," I said.

"Skip the pineapple this time," Ralph said.

I didn't tell him that I was going to try raisins next.

Chapter Seven

"My mother says sweets are bad for you," Briney said the next afternoon. "But thanks anyway."

She wouldn't even touch the plate of brownies I offered her.

How could anyone not eat brownies? Especially ones with raisins?

"As long as you're here, you can stay," Briney said. "I thought you might be with that Ralph kid. He's awfully young."

"Only a year younger than I am," I said. But I didn't want to talk about Ralph. I had come to find out more about Briney.

"Maybe you'd like to see my dog," she said.

I left the brownies by the front door and followed Briney outside. The dog barked and pulled at his chain. But when Briney walked up to him, he licked her face.

"His name is Sam," Briney said, rubbing him behind his ears. "You can pet him if you want."

I put out my hand slowly, and Sam rubbed his nose into it.

"My mother says he's too big to be in the house," Briney said. Her voice softened a little. "I wish he could sleep in my room."

I guess this was another of her mother's rules. I felt sort of sorry for her. Krista's mother had always let Sparky sleep on Krista's bed.

Briney kissed Sam on his nose and turned around.

"Come into the living room," she said to

me. I followed her back into the house.

The living room looked stiff and cold. When Krista had lived there, it always looked cozy. I noticed a big piano in the corner.

"You sit over there," Briney said, pointing to an uncomfortable-looking chair.

I sat down, and Briney sat down at the piano and began to play. I was surprised. She was good. I tried tapping my foot, but it wasn't foot-tapping music. It was slow. And sad. I listened carefully, though. When Briney was done, I clapped.

The next song was slower. And sadder. Soon, I lost count of how many songs Briney played. My chair got harder and harder.

Finally, Briney stood up and bowed.

"You'd better go now," she said. "I have to feed Sam. You can listen to me play again tomorrow."

Listening to more sad music didn't sound

like fun. Nothing with Briney seemed like fun.

"Uh . . . I'll ask my mother if I can," I said. And I took my brownies and left.

On my way home, I wondered how I could get out of having to go back there. Maybe Mom would tell me I had to clean the house from top to bottom.

If I was lucky.

Chapter Eight

Ralph was waiting for me when I got home. I told him about Briney while he scraped the brownie crumbs from the baking pan.

"Sounds like she wanted an audience," Ralph said.

"She asked me back tomorrow," I said.

"And you want to go?" he asked.

I didn't really. Not if I had to listen to Briney play the piano again.

"Her dog is nice," I said. I told Ralph all about Sam.

"It's too bad Briney's not as nice to people as she is to her dog," Ralph said.

I sighed. If Briney was going to be my friend, I would have to go tomorrow. Why couldn't Briney be like Krista or Ralph? We always did fun things together.

Ralph picked out a raisin from the crumbs and tossed it into the trash can.

"I guess this means you're friends now," Ralph said.

"I guess so," I said.

I knew what this meant. Ralph followed me to my room, and I took down the Oxy-Morons poster.

"Here," I said to Ralph, rolling up the poster. "You've earned it."

I followed him back into the kitchen. I hated to give away my favorite poster, but I had agreed. Mom looked at me.

"Ralph's taught you a lot about making friends," she said. "But sometimes people just don't fit with each other."

"But Briney lives so close," I said. "Right where Krista lived. And she has a dog like Krista's. And she's got long hair, just like Krista's."

"But she isn't Krista," Mom reminded me. "You and Krista fit."

"Briney and I fit *just fine*," I said, and I stamped my foot, just a little. "I'm not going to complain about her. She's my only friend."

"I'd better be going," Ralph said in a low voice. He walked quickly toward the back door.

"I'll make your brownies tomorrow," I called after him. The door closed and I heard him run down the steps.

"Why did he leave so fast?" I asked.

Mom didn't answer.

For the first time all summer, Ralph hadn't tried to stand on his head. Dad would say he was getting some sense. Mom would say something was wrong.

Why did everything seem so mixed up?

Chapter
Nine

"I'm glad you're here," Briney said the next afternoon.

She pulled me into her house. Maybe this was going to work out after all.

"I am, too," I said. "I brought a video game. It's really good."

"Never mind that," Briney said. "I have a wonderful idea. I'm starting a club. I'll be the president, of course. And since you're the only one I know around here so far, you'll be the vice president."

It really was a great idea. Krista and I had never had a club.

"When school starts, we'll get other kids to join," Briney said. "Of course, we'll be careful who we let in."

"Ralph can be in charge of membership," I said. "He'll be good at getting people. He knows everyone."

Briney looked at me in amazement. "We're *not* going to let Ralph in the club," she said. "He's too young. And he's a boy. And besides, he's funny-looking."

"He isn't funny-looking," I said. I stopped. "Well, maybe he is, a little, but he's fun and friendly and—"

"He's a little squirt who hangs around because he can't get friends of his own," Briney said.

I felt my face get hot. Briney might be nice to her dog, but Ralph was right. She wasn't so good with people.

"That's not true," I said. "He has plenty of

friends. Everyone who meets him likes him."

"I don't," Briney said, tossing her hair. "And if you want to be friends with *me*, you can't keep hanging around with *him*."

I stared at Briney. How could I give up Ralph? We liked the same things. We talked a lot. We had fun together. It would be like giving up Krista.

My mouth was dry and my face burned. But this time I got the words out, all on my own.

"I wouldn't give up Ralph for you," I said. "I don't want to join your club. And I don't want to be your friend."

Then I ran out of Briney's house.

Chapter Ten

I had tried so hard to be friends with Briney. Now she'd never talk to me again.

Down deep, I really didn't care. But school was starting soon, and Krista lived far away.

When Ralph came over the next day, he had a rolled-up poster in his hand.

"Your brownies are on the counter," I said.

"What's in them?" Ralph asked, taking one and looking at it carefully.

"A-N," I said.

"Applesauce and Nuts?" he asked, looking disappointed.

"Absolutely Nothing," I said.

Ralph grinned and took a bite.

"How'd it go with Briney?" Ralph asked.

I couldn't lie to Ralph.

"Awful," I said. "She's rude and mean and unfriendly."

"What happened?" he asked, surprised.

I shrugged. There were some things Ralph shouldn't know.

"We just don't . . . fit," I said.

"Then it's a good thing I brought back the poster," he said.

He stuffed a second brownie in his mouth.

"But it was part of our deal," I said.

"But you and Briney aren't friends. That was the deal," he said. "Besides, I'm not going to take your favorite poster. Friends don't do things like that to each other."

I stared at him, and then I smiled. Ralph had been my friend all along, and I didn't even know it.

"Let's go outside," Ralph said. "I want to practice H-S."

"Head Stands," I said, and laughed. I finally got one right. And I had the feeling that this time Ralph would really do one.

"Never mind Briney Manelli," I said. "I guess I have a friend to walk to school with after all."

About the Author

Lynea Bowdish likes reading children's books almost as much as she likes writing them. Originally from Brooklyn and Long Island, Lynea lives in Hollywood, Maryland, with her husband, David Roberts, and two dogs, Chipper and Princess. Chipper has already appeared in one book. Princess and David are waiting for their turns. Lynea's other PAGES Publishing Group titles include *Downey and Buttercup*; *Downey and Buttercup's Adventure*; and *Too-Too Justin*.

About the Artist

Meredith Johnson works as an art director creating lots and lots of TV commercials for Barbie® and Ken®. But she really likes to draw pictures for kids' books best. Meredith and her husband Larre live in Flintridge, California, with their two children Matt and Casey.

Cathie Dunsford has taught literature at Auckland University, was Fulbright Post-Doctoral Research Scholar at the University of Berkeley from 1984 to 1986 and has directed three New Zealand Writers' Conferences. In 1992 Cathie Dunsford completed a lecture tour of Europe, England and the USA and International Feminist Book Fairs in Montreal and Amsterdam.

Her own writing has appeared in publications in the USA, Canada, England, Australia and New Zealand. A bi-lingual collection of her poetry, *Survivors: Uberlebende* was published by the University of Osnabrück Press, Germany in 1990. She has edited many collections of writing, including the New Women's Fiction Series. Her latest anthology, *Me and Marilyn Monroe*, published by Daphne Brasell Associates Press (NZ) challenges the war against women's bodies through fiction.

Cathie Dunsford is director of Dunsford and Associates Publishing Consultants – a feminist owned and run company which searches for, assesses, edits and sells feminist texts to the publishing industry. She currently teaches Creative Writing and Publishing at the University of Auckland, New Zealand.

COWRIE

Cathie Dunsford

Spinifex Press Pty Ltd
504 Queensberry Street
North Melbourne Vic 3051
Australia

First published by Spinifex Press 1994

Typeset in Sabon by Claire Warren
Cover design by Liz Nicholson, Design Bite
Production by Morgan Blackthorne Productions
Printed in Australia by Australian Print Group

National Library of Australia
Cataloguing-in-Publication entry:
CIP

Dunsford, Cathie, 1953–   .

    Cowrie.

    ISBN 1 875559 28 0

    I. Title.

NZ823.2

For Audre Lorde, who took the time to work with me on the first draft, Berlin, August 1992, when she was in the final weeks of her battle with cancer. Her last words to me were to extract a promise to finish the novel. Audre named her hei matau "Cowrie" in honour of the text and Gloria Joseph returned the bone carving for me to wear while working on the final draft.

Mahalo, Audre. I hope you are pleased with the outcome. Thanks for your honesty, insight and love. I miss you.

ACKNOWLEDGEMENTS

Mahalo to:

Herb Kawainui Kane, for his inspiration and permission to use his superb Pele painting for the cover. Martha Beckwith and Katherine Luolama, for adding to my knowledge of Pele and Laukiamanuikahiki. Dr Trina Nahm-Mijo, University of Hawai'i, Hilo, Fay Hovey – Volcano Arts Centre; Diane Aki; Jessie and Hanoa; Pele Aloha; Karen Anne (Maui); Andrei Codrescu – Hawai'i, Hawai'ian Petroglyphs, H. Cox, E. Stasack, Bishop Museum, Hawai'i. Beryl Fletcher, Susan Sayer, Daphne Brasell, Geoff Walker, Susan Hawthorne, Renate Klein, Michelle Proctor, Keri Hulme and Doreen Dunsford – all of whom contributed comments at draft stages of writing. Special thanks for the support of the Broomsbury Writers, Powhiri Rika-Heke and Dr Sigrid Markmann; Orlanda Frauenverlag, Audre Lorde and Gloria Joseph for their encouragement in Berlin; Spinifex Press, especially Susan Hawthorne, Renate Klein and Michelle Proctor; and Tandem Press – Helen Benton and Bob Ross in Aotearoa.

Arohanui, Aloha

– Cath Dunsford, Tawharanui, May, 1994.

A settlement rises out of the lava rocks and around the lagoon. Voices and wind rustle through the coconut trees. She is floating on the waves, far out at sea. There is a distant rumbling. Water whips up around her, lashing her body. A strong current drags her out, sends her skimming back at rocket speed, seaweed smashing into her face, her shell. She is reeling on the wind, over the sea, high above the land. The ocean is on her tail, flying with her through the air. She exalts in its freedom, flings her small fins outward and screams.

"There, there, Cowrie. Auatu. Mere is here. The wave won't drown you. Besides, there are no coconut trees in Aotearoa. It's in your imagination. You are a strong swimmer. You can enter back into the wave. It does not have to eat you up."

A dash of sand hits Cowrie's face as children run by and she sits up, wondering why her recurring childhood nightmare has followed her to the shores of Punalu'u, Hawai'i.

Cowrie touches the coconut etching twinned to the bone hei matau Mere gave her before leaving home. She remembers fingering its soft edges as a child and dreaming of a woman who could live in the sea protected by her dark brown shell, a woman who would skim the waves to shore and dive back through them to the waiting ocean. But sometimes the dreams would turn to nightmares. Mere would always be there to comfort her.

She digs her toes into the hot, black sand of Punalu'u Beach beside an oval lagoon fringed by coconut trees and a thatched hut housing local artifacts. Cowrie has not been inside yet. At the far end of the beach, the remains of a stone heiau or temple which she'd explored earlier. Ahead, the glistening calm ocean. In the distance, a line of people streaming in from a tourist bus to the thatched hut behind the lagoon. She places her towel and water bottle in her pack and begins walking up towards the village at Pahala.

Crowds file into the small museum to see the mural painted by Herb Kawainui Kane. It features Punalu'u as it might have been two centuries earlier when the beach housed a village of thatched huts. Women prepare food under the shade of the trees while men work on the canoes. At the far end of the beach a heiau, Kane'ele'ele, rises up out of the sea-spray like a vision. The mural is painted on a magnificent curved wall, as long as an ancient canoe, as high as a coconut tree, and reinforced against earthquakes.

The guide explains that the painting depicts Punalu'u Beach village and heiau which was destroyed by a tsunami in 1868. Later, a twenty-foot wave rose up over the beach crashing down upon the museum they stand in now, destroying everything and pushing mud knee high up the wall. But the mural, which extends to floor level, was completely untouched. A tourist asks how this can be so. The guide shakes his head and says, "It is protected." He does not tell how his grandmother had seen a giant sea turtle with the head of a woman at the peak of the wave as it surged upwards. How the turtle had dived back into the wave and remained, far out at sea, looking over the beach protectively until the storm was over.

Keo and Paneke live in one of the old sugar cane houses on a plantation high above Pahala. The journey up through the macadamia plantation is hazardous. Large rocks from the plantation trucks stud the road and driving is slow. Cowrie's old truck weaves drunkenly around the mounds and rattles with each change of direction. Macadamia groves turn into waving stalks of sugar cane and soon the truck is dwarfed by the massive plants.

She swerves to avoid a mound in the road ahead. A huge, beautifully sculpted rock, glistening in the sun, appears to move slightly to the left. Cowrie takes off her sunglasses for a better look. She drives to the right of the mound and it moves again. She hauls on the brakes and jumps out. The mound is a large land turtle. Its head disappears inside its shell as soon as she approaches.

What a beauty, she thinks, and places her hand on its warm back. The turtle remains stone still, but her hand is jolted off its back. It is as if an electric charge has entered her. She falls against the side of the truck, gasping, then stares at the turtle, dazed. This is not the protective creature who swims through her dreams. Her wet hand on the hot shell has acted as a shock conductor. Despite her prodding, the turtle remains inside its shell. It has no intention of moving. Cowrie climbs back into the cab and veers around the obstacle.

The road narrows at the top of the sugar cane plantation and turns left into a dirt track. Husky brown fern trunks spring from the roadside and their lush green and silver leaves fan out in a canopy above her. Suddenly, the heavens open. The leaves shiver and flicker with the weight of the water flowing down their spines. Below, ginger flowers gorge on the falling water, turning it to sweet scented honey as it runs down the shimmering leaves and trickles on to the black earth.

Drops pour on to her left arm and shoulder, tickling her breasts and shoulder blades through the lavalava and she enjoys their sensual flow. In the rain, she can just make out a building ahead to the right. It looks too large for the cottage. Closer up, she sees it is some kind of temple, painted red and yellow, with a red, yellow, green and white flag hoisted up a pole at the entrance way.

She continues until the track veers left down towards an old wooden barn decorated with washboards, rusty farm implements and a magnificent stark white goat's head. A fresh frangipani lei hangs from the horns in welcome. Cousin Keo said to watch out for the barn with the goat's head at the entrance. Beyond it is a charmingly dilapidated old, green cottage with wooden shutters. The truck swings in between the cottage and the barn, coming to a halt in front of a lush patch of taro. She decides to leave her kete of kalo and uala she'd bought to go with the meal, inside the truck. They have plenty here. But she grabs the feijoa wine and jumps down on to the rocky path.

A round-bellied Hawai'ian man emerges from the back of the cottage. Cowrie is amazed to see the likeness to her grandfather's picture in the old Kodak box. Only here, a much softer version. Keo takes down the lei from the goat's horns and places it around her neck.

"Aloha, hoahanau." He touches her nose with his. She returns the greeting.

"Haele mai, meet Paneke." Keo leads Cowrie to the back of the cottage and she drops off her jandals in the row of shoes outside the door.

Paneke greets them. "Aloha, Cowrie. Please come inside." She wraps a huge, brown arm around Cowrie's waist and draws her into the kitchen.

It reminds her of farm kitchens in Tai Tokerau. She feels right at home. Scrubbed wooden walls and tools hanging off nails. At the end, a large, wooden table with benches either side. In the middle of the table, a vase of fresh ginger which engulfs the room with its sweet, sickly fragrance.

After drinks of fresh pineapple and coconut over ice, and many laughs and inquisitive searchings of each other's cultures, Keo lifts kai from the umu and they sit down to the meal. "Fresh 'ahi caught this morning and baked in banana leaves," explains Keo, unfolding the leaves.

Cowrie stiffens in shock. She knows that locals used to eat turtles, but dolphins?

Paneke notices her shock. "You don't like fish?" she asks.

Cowrie takes a deep breath. "I love it. But 'ahi, dolphin?"

Paneke and Keo burst into laughter. "Dolphin is mahi-mahi, not 'ahi," Paneke explains.

Beside the 'ahi are kalo and uala, wrapped in kalo leaves.

"That flavours the vegetable and helps the sap to stay in," explains Paneke.

Between each dish is a bowl of poi. It is purple with a texture like yoghurt. The flavour is delicate. She asks how it is made.

"It's kalo beaten to a pulp," explains Paneke.

The poi is delicious, but it is the 'ahi soaked in banana leaves that most appeals to her. The smell is smoky and sweet. The moisture of the fresh fish is retained and the banana leaf adds a subtle taste.

Paneke asks how Cowrie found them.

Cowrie explains that when Mere adopted her from the Rawene Orphanage, all she had with her was an old Kodak box containing a cowrie shell, a turtle etched on a piece of coconut and a yellowed newspaper article recounting a tsunami in 1868. Once Cowrie had completed her studies,

Mere urged her to write to the address scrawled across the back of the cutting: Kini Aloha, c/- Na'alehu Post Office, Hawai'i and she'd received a reply from Kini's grand-daughter, Koana, inviting her to come and stay and explaining that one of Cowrie's relatives, Keo, still worked on the sugar cane plantation at Pahala.

Keo wants to know what it was like growing up in Aotearoa without true knowledge of her origin.

Cowrie explains it wasn't so bad after Mere took her from the orphanage. But she still felt like an outsider. She was lighter-skinned than Mere's other children but darker than the Pakeha school kids. She was neither Maori nor Pakeha – an alien – and compensated for this by trying to fit in all the time. She worked twice as hard for half as much. Being called a "fat Polynesian" at school didn't help. Even her name, after the cowrie shell in Apelahama's box, marked her as different. Mere said she'd grow to be strong like Tane Mahuta, God of the kauri forest.

"Strong enough for my treat?" asks Keo, opening up the huge, ancient fridge that rumbles away contentedly in the corner. He takes out a large, oval watermelon which has been sliced in half. Inside is a mountain of fresh fruit: pineapple, watermelon, mango . . . Cowrie feels the juices rising in her.

"Hala-kahiki, ipu, manako . . . come, eat," says Keo, holding out a bowl made from a coconut shell.

Cowrie takes the coconut half from his hand and is about to ladle fresh fruit into its shell when she notices a carving on the inside. A turtle with a woman on its back, coasting over the waves. She is startled. It is the turtle-woman she has been dreaming about. She holds the carved bowl out to Keo, pointing to its interior.

"Who is this, Keo?"

Keo smiles. "Ah, that is Laukiamanuikahiki. She was brought up on Kauai without knowledge of her origin. She rides a turtle."

"She rides a turtle. That means she's still swimming in

6

the ocean around us?"

"Could be," says Keo, winking at Paneke. "You seen her, Cowrie?"

Cowrie smiles. "What if I have, Keo?"

Keo grunts. "You keep away from her, girl. She burnt down her brother's house. She has strong powers." For a moment he looks serious, then he breaks into a high-pitched contralto laugh. "Just watch you don't eat her," he adds, screaming with laughter.

Cowrie enjoys the thought, but not as Keo means it.

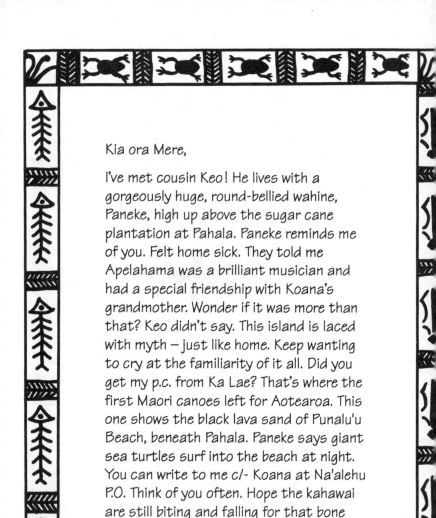

Kia ora Mere,

I've met cousin Keo! He lives with a gorgeously huge, round-bellied wahine, Paneke, high up above the sugar cane plantation at Pahala. Paneke reminds me of you. Felt home sick. They told me Apelahama was a brilliant musician and had a special friendship with Koana's grandmother. Wonder if it was more than that? Keo didn't say. This island is laced with myth – just like home. Keep wanting to cry at the familiarity of it all. Did you get my p.c. from Ka Lae? That's where the first Maori canoes left for Aotearoa. This one shows the black lava sand of Punalu'u Beach, beneath Pahala. Paneke says giant sea turtles surf into the beach at night. You can write to me c/- Koana at Na'alehu P.O. Think of you often. Hope the kahawai are still biting and falling for that bone and paua trace I made you. Think of me eating raw 'ahi drenched in limes – yum!

Arohanui – Cowrie.

Cowrie lies on her back in the still water. Above her, the giant mamaku stretch out over the bay. She feels a ripple as something swims under her. A sweet smell fills her nostrils. She is woken by giggles and laughter. Koana's daughter, Nele, is holding a freshly peeled segment of mango over her face, willing her to wake up and play. Her brother, Peni, laughs gleefully as she bites into the mango and pretends to take Nele's finger also. Nele screams with delight and Koana appears at the door to see what all the fuss is about.

"It's ok, Koana. Time I got up anyway."

Koana shoos the kids away and sits down on the old cane chair beside the hammock, strung between the back porch uprights, where Cowrie sleeps.

"What did Keo tell you about your grandfather, Cowrie?"

"Not too much. He was a bit of an old devil, evidently. But sounds like he got on pretty well with your grandmother, Ko!"

"Yeah, but I think they were just close friends."

"Often the best relationships, eh? Well, it seems that Apelahama worked for a US outfit, stringing 'ukulele. When the firm opened up a music shop in New Zealand, they asked Apelahama if he'd go. It was just after his home had been destroyed by the lava-flow, so he thought, why not, and went. All he had with him was an old Kodak box and the clothes he stood up in. When in New Zealand, he met and married a kiwi woman, Leonie, and they had my birth mum, Laura."

"But I thought your mum was Mere?"

"Well, she is, to me. Laura gave me up when her boyfriend left her. She couldn't manage alone. Mere adopted me from the orphanage at Rawene."

"So what does Keo think about having a kiwi cousin?"

"I reckon he's quite pleased, actually. I really like him and Paneke, and they've invited me back any time. They wanted me to stay with them, but I think I should find my own place to live."

"The hammock getting a bit much, eh?" Koana laughs.

"Na. Used to it. I often go kayaking and camping in Aotearoa. Besides, I always feel like I'm floating when in a hammock, and that's as near to bliss as possible for me."

"Turtle woman rides the waves."

"Who's she?" asks Cowrie, interested in how much Koana knows about her.

"You," laughs Koana, and pulls the hammock way out to the left so it swings wildly back again. Cowrie grabs her on the return swing and pulls her into the hammock. Koana is on top of her. They grapple, each trying to tickle the other until they are both weak with laughter. The hammock is still for a moment. Koana looks down into her eyes. Cowrie wants to reach up and touch her cheek, her lips. Koana smiles gently.

Peni rushes back into the room and grabs Koana's arm. "Mama, mama, Aka here. Aka here." Peni runs back to greet his father and Koana sighs, slips off the hammock and goes to the door.

They talk in Hawai'ian and Cowrie can only pick up a few words that are similar to Maori. Locals here say that Ka Lae, the southern-most tip of the Big Island of Hawai'i, is the point from which the ancient canoes left for Aotearoa. Cowrie knows that her ancestors were superb navigators, but the distance between Hawai'i and Aotearoa seems so vast, even for the mighty waka they built.

Koana brings Aka out on to the back porch. She introduces them and says Aka has offered to take the kids fishing and would she like to go too?

"Are you going, Koana?"

"Sure. I love fishing."

"Then count me in," says Cowrie, leaping out of the hammock on to the wooden floorboards with a thunderous crash.

Even Aka laughs. "You'd make ok local wahine," he exclaims.

Koana slaps him across the buttocks with her hand. "You keep away from kiwi wahine, Aka. She's my friend."

Cowrie blushes. She is delighted that Koana protects her in this way. "Where are you going fishing, Aka?"

"Just here. No transport. I had to hitch a ride to Na'alehu," he grins.

"What's it like fishing at Ka Lae? I'd love to go there."

"Kamaha'o. Wonderful. But it's too far to walk!"

"Well, let's go in the old truck. The kids love it."

"How did you know about Ka Lae?"

"The local storekeeper told me that this is where the canoes departed for Aotearoa – New Zealand. So I'd like to see the place."

"I've heard that too," admits Aka. "But how could they have gone that far? It must've been a miracle."

"I reckon it was, but one aided by superb navigational skills that took Polynesians all over the Pacific."

"Well, let's see if you kiwis are as good at fishing as your ancestors, then." Aka throws his nets and lines into the back of the truck, parked below the porch. The kids are already in the tray, pretending to be hauling huge monsters out of the sea, gouging out their eyes and eating them.

Cowrie laughs, remembering how she used to show the visitors who came into the bay at summer how to gut fish. She particularly enjoyed showing off in front of the bigger boys. She'd make a clean slice down the belly and cut the tendons holding the guts in as she swept back up the fish with one gesture, then her chubby hand would pull out the gut, blood dripping between her fingers. If there was roe in the belly, she'd eat it raw. Then she'd gouge out the eyes and hand them to the boys, making them eat the blood-soaked balls. They were so protective of their fragile egos that they always did as she said. The girls would shriek in terror, but still watch, fascinated. Then they'd avoid the boys who'd eaten the eyes because their breath stank all day.

The young Cowrie reckoned it was good to have a gutting session at the very beginning of the holiday season so that it established her as the one to whom all fish would come for their final rituals. After the ceremony, the kids would be so revolted, she'd usually end up with most of the fish they'd caught. It also served to keep the boys at bay for the rest of the holiday and the girls stayed in awe of her skills. That suited her fine.

Peni grabs Cowrie's arm. "Mai, mai," he yells. Cowrie reaches for her lavalava. She throws her pack into the tray, lifts Peni back up and climbs into the cab beside Koana. Aka jumps in on the starboard side. Cowrie revs up the engine, sending the kids into screams of glee, and shoves her into gear. She finds using her right hand to do this awkward. Koana seems to sense this and touches her arm lightly. Cowrie smiles, enjoying her closeness.

The road winds around the Big Island beside the sea. Cowrie loves it. So like the West Coast of the South Island. From Okarito to Westport. Rugged, grey rocks streaked with horizontal sepia lines. Wild pounamu sea smashing against the jagged spires, curving and moulding them to the gothic shapes of its imagination. One of the rock formations reminds her of Punakaiki, dubbed the Pancake Rocks by tourists who saw them layered upon each other in huge piles. Cowrie could almost see the heavens opening, and cascades of maple syrup rolling down the layers of rock.

"Maybe you'll come and visit our coast sometime, eh?"

"Maybe one day, Cowrie. But the airfare is more than we earn in a year," adds Koana.

"Yeah, but it'll be better if they put the satellite in. More jobs," says Aka.

Koana glares at him. She starts yelling in Hawai'ian. All Cowrie can pick up is "fucking American trash." Then there is silence. She asks what the satellite is. Koana replies that NASA wants to establish a satellite station at Ka Lae, on the southern tip of Hawai'i and has promised the locals plenty of jobs and a boost to the tourist trade if it goes ahead. She feels they are being bribed. "First they take over our land and we have to buy it back from them, then they want it for their space programme. It's just high tech spying, really. And then they'll use us to test their nuclear weapons . . . "

"That's already happening on Kaho'olawe," chips in Aka. "The Americans took over the island, have destroyed the heiau and have desecrated our sacred land. They test their weapons on the surface and underwater. It's meant that we have to be careful where we fish these days. We know they do harm but we need jobs also. Once we could rely on our fishing for income, now we are reliant on them. It stinks. Yet I need a job to help support Koana and the kids, and while I don't want the satellite station, I reckon it's better than a nuclear power plant."

"Not much difference, Aka. We'll still be the target for any foreign invasion. We must keep our islands free of this madness. We must not give in to them," pleads Koana, tears filling her eyes.

Cowrie wants to reach out and hold her. But she resists. Lucky she needs both arms to drive this old beast. She is appalled. She tells Koana and Aka of the US invasion of the Marshall Islands, which they do not know about, and how the scientists took the islanders from their sacred birthplace and relocated them on other islands. They used their sacred island for testing nuclear devices. Then, when they had finished, they covered one island with concrete half a mile thick and told the islanders that they could move back to their original island at their own risk.

The New Zealand Greenpeace boat, the *Rainbow Warrior*, had intervened to help the islanders. That's why the French wanted to bomb her. Now, the islanders were suffering the after-effects: children being born with three arms, two heads and sometimes without limbs at all. They were called 'jellyfish babies'.

Before Cowrie can finish, Koana touches her arm. "That is enough, Cowrie. I cannot bear to hear more. You see, Aka. It's not so simple as just finding jobs. You want Nele and Peni's kids to be jellyfish babies? No, we can't go that way, nor can we return to what was. We have to find other ways of surviving, but on our terms."

They drive in silence, until they hear the kids yelling from the tray and pointing to their left. A long road, not much more than a dirt track, leads down towards the sea. Aka says it's Ka Lae, so she swings the wheel hard left and turns on to the bumpy track. On both sides of the road are windmills that generate electricity for the island. Further down, the surface turns into lava rock. Beyond this, a massive ledge surges out over the Pacific with a vertical drop to the echoing sea.

They walk out to the edge of the cliffs in silence. Below are canoes and old wooden boats, tied to the sides of the cliff. Foot-holes and dilapidated ladders mark the cliff-face. The sea is treacherous. One man brings a canoe up alongside his ladder and skillfully grabs the rope. The tide disappears beneath him as the wave swells back out again. He holds the canoe between his feet, dangling from the rope ladder and waits for the next wave to lift the canoe upwards. He grabs its prow rope and ties it up to the ladder, then begins the slow ascent up the vertical rock, his sack of fish tied on to his back. Cowrie holds her breath, praying he will make it. No worries. He's up and over the edge in less than two minutes.

"Aloha, Vile," yells Aka. He goes over and they speak rapidly in Hawai'ian. Then Aka brings Vile back and introduces him to Cowrie.

"Vile met a kiwi once. Liked him. You tell her, Vile," says Aka.

Vile looks shy, takes the load off his back, sits down on the edge of the cliff and pulls out some tobacco. He rolls two cigarettes, lights one off the other and hands the second to Aka. By now, they are all sitting down, legs over the edge, listening. Vile takes his time. He enjoys a good story. He tells them how he met a fella from Tai Tokerau, Aotearoa. A Maori fella. He and his mates were fishing off a big outrigger they'd sailed over. They called it Ngeru. Both hulls were the same width. Not a canoe with a rigger. Anyway, they had a bit of weed one night and a few drinks and the question of the yankees testing their nuclear weapons on Hawai'ian soil came up. When the kiwi fella heard about this use of the sacred island, he got real mad and suggested they return to the island and rebuild the heiau, the sacred temple, with stones. The locals explained that the island was guarded by the US military and could not be landed on. The kiwi fella said so was Greenham Common guarded, yet his wife and a bunch of pommy sheilas had got in and painted the silos with peace symbols.

"We planned to try to land on the island the next night. We couldn't get near enough, so we anchored out and swam to shore. We each took a large rock and began building up the stone heiau, with Koma leading us. We worked all night. We did this for several weeks until the heiau was complete. On the last night, we lit a fire in cele-bration. That's when the guards came. They fired bullets at us as we swam back to the boat. But we succeeded. We rebuilt the temple, stone by stone."

"Is it still there?" asks Peni.

"No, Peni. They blasted it apart. We saw the flames as we headed back out. Some thought it was the yanks. Others thought it was Pele blowing it up in their faces. But it was a good feeling to have done it. And the kiwi fella helped. A good bro." He laughed, but Cowrie could see the pain in his face. It was a great victory under the circumstances, but it would have to be done over and over again before it had its effect on the soldiers, before it wore them down. Then Cowrie notices him smiling. She wonders if the retelling of the story has the effect of reinventing the struggle, giving it more force each time it is told.

"Let's go fishing," cries Nele at her elbow.

Cowrie sees Aka crawling to his feet and farewelling his friend. They walk in silence back from the cliff-face of Ka Lae, bearing its ancient secrets in their hearts, along with these more recent tales.

Tena koe Kuini

Finally reached the big island: Hawai'i. So like home: my
Rangitoto and your Whakarewarewa combined. Still active
volcano at Kilauea with Hawai'ian Goddess, Pele, inside.
She emits an awesome power! Staying with delicious
Koana — mokopuna of Tutu Kini, friend of my grandfather,
Apelahama. She's stunning, with delightful twins, Nele and
Peni. We get on well as whanau. But also feel attraction for
Koana. Having to hold back for now. You know what it's like,
nei? Need to suss out the rellies first.

Remember Bastion Point? Same issues here — only the
yanks want to build a satellite station on native land at
Ka Lae (sacred leaving point of waka for Aotearoa).
They've already destroyed one island, but the locals rebuilt
their temple (heiau) after it was desecrated by the US
military. Met some fishermen who told me a Ngapuhi fella
in a rigger called Ngeru helped them out. One of your
rellies, no doubt! (You're lucky you can claim your Ngapuhi
or Tainui whakapapa, depending on the occasion. Good
insurance, eh?)

How's things at home — and the university? Have they
learned to appreciate your treaty work yet? Yeah — and
pigs might fly! Love to the Waikato Writing Group — and
heaps more for you.

Arohanui — Cowrie XXX

PS: See these amazing hula dancers with gourds, animals
I've sketched on border. They're from ancient rock carvings
— pre Pakeha (haole here!) Koana promises to take me to
see some later.

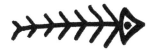

The fishing expedition is a success. Mostly 'ula'ula, snapper, but some interesting small fish in the net which Peni and Nele delight in. They seemed to like the huge variety of papa'i, crabs, which they name for Cowrie: a'ama, 'elemihi, 'alamihi, ohiki, unauna, 'ala'eke, mo'ala and kohunu. Peni likes the ohiki best, Nele, the a'ama. Cowrie votes for the kohunu. All are gathered, cleaned and roasted over an old piece of corrugated iron on the beach. She could be in Aotearoa. She writes home about the fishing trip, her grandfather and Vile's tale of rebuilding the heiau. But she does not mention her feelings for Koana. That can wait.

Koana is back at work in the Na'alehu Post Office and Keo is preparing tracks in the sugar cane fields, so Cowrie calls Paneke who says she must visit Pele. Locals talk about the volcano goddess as a real, living being. She's heard the shopkeepers mention Pele and has read enough about her since arriving to know that she is not a woman to be messed around with. A Hawai'ian Hinekaro.

Paneke suggests that they start out early and walk through the crater at Kilauea before it gets too hot. Cowrie is alarmed, but excited, by the idea of actually descending into the crater. She knows it is still active. Paneke assures her she has taken visitors through the crater before but they must visit Pele first and ask for her protection. Only locals know the correct path. One foot out of place and you're into an underground lava flow.

Soon after their conversation, the old truck, which Nele named Honu after Cowrie told her of the turtle on the road to Keo's place, is rattling up through Volcano National Park, coughing and spluttering as it crawls higher and higher up the slopes of Kilauea. Cowrie is discovering that Paneke is more talkative away from Keo. She knows so much about Pele and the history of the volcano.

Honu just makes it to the top of the rise and then the road flattens out to reveal a huge crater. Honu's wheels are nearly on the rim and Cowrie stops to get out for a better look. Paneke tells her to wait until they reach the next crater, Hale ma'uma'u, where Pele currently lives.

They park some distance from the rim and Paneke takes Cowrie over the road and into the bush. They are dwarfed by giant mamaku and a tree that looks just like pohutukawa. Paneke explains that it is the 'ohi'a tree and the blossom is lehua. Cowrie reaches to pick a lehua blossom to examine it more closely. Paneke grabs her arm, just before she snaps off the scarlet explosion. Cowrie is shocked at the power of her action.

"Mai, uoki!" shouts Paneke. "A'ole!"

Cowrie retracts her hand as if scolded by hot lava.

Paneke looks her directly in the eye. "I don't mean to frighten you, Cowrie. But you must understand. Hina-ulu-'ohi'a is the female goddess of the 'ohi'a-lehua forest. In the shape of the 'ohi'a tree she protects Hi'i-lawe, child of Kakea and Kaholo and Lau-ka-ieie, daughter of Po-kahi. To both god and goddess the flowering 'ohi'a is sacred and it is forbidden for anyone travelling to the smoking volcano to take the blood-red flowers or even to gather leaves or branches."

Cowrie doesn't want to invoke the wrath of the gods.

Paneke takes her hand. "It's ok, Cowrie. We'll come here on the way home. It's acceptable to gather these blossoms on the return journey, after I have invoked the gods and goddesses. I will show you how to make a lehua wreath to crown your head when we've been through the crater."

Cowrie smiles tentatively. If we get through the crater. She asks Paneke what would have happened if she had taken the blossom. Paneke replies that the punishment is always different, depending on the intention of the traveller, that she has brought Cowrie into the forest beside the crater to pick 'ohelo berries to offer to Pele so their journey through the crater is a peaceful one.

After gathering the blood-red berries, Paneke takes her across the hardened lava to a place on the rim of Hale ma'uma'u. She invokes Pele in a ritual and together they cast the 'ohelo berries over the side and down into the vast cavern of the crater. The berry gifts glide downwards until Cowrie can only see black dots before they reach the crater floor. Paneke's call sounds like a karanga with that soul-piercing cry which feels like it comes from another planet. Its echoes resound through her body, electrifying every part of her flesh and bones and entering her soul. They wait after each call, until it descends into the crater, shimmers across the hallowed cavern and bounces back off the far wall.

Pele has answered them.

Paneke smiles, and gestures to Cowrie that they can now begin the journey.

They walk around the rim of Hale ma'uma'u, feeling the presence of Pele within. It is eerie and exciting. Cowrie is amazed at how Pele has moved and shifted the land at her whim. As they begin the descent into the crater, the heat from the lava-rocks rolls up at them in waves. She notices small ferns poking out of crevices in the older lava and is fascinated by their survival. The further down they go, the higher the rim rises until they are finally on the crater floor, dwarfed by the massive walls.

Cowrie follows Paneke's footsteps carefully. The cracked lava and steam vents make the crater resemble the surface of the moon. She recalls those first photographs relayed back to earth. A crusty planet of rock with human figures bouncing over it in slow motion. The heat makes her lightheaded and she imagines her steps are huge leaps slowed down by video replay.

Paneke turns to make sure Cowrie is directly behind her. She appears so distant. Her face is serene and calm. She smiles gently. Her large body gracefully weaves between the rocks like a dolphin in water. Cowrie remembers a dream where she felt a sensation like this. She was on a barque guided by a black cat and as they moved towards the entrance of a giant cave inside an island, her oar became redundant and the barque was drawn by a force that seemed to come from within the cave. A dark cloud moved over them and then she heard a strange and haunting noise. Looking up, she realised it was the slow wingbeat of a huge bird that looked like a pterodactyl. The bird opened its beak and a shower of silver and blue fish descended on them.

"Ouch!" Cowrie stubs her toe on a thick outcrop of rock. The lava forms a skin over the land and there is a flesh-coloured reddy-brown in some of the seams. One wall of lava has solidified like strands of rope, each inter-woven with the next, so that the ropes run in a vertical pattern along the shelf. Others form semi-circles that embrace each other, like rows of lovers lying tucked around the one in front. Each lava flow has a story to tell.

By now, sweat is pouring from both of them. Cowrie can taste the saltiness of her skin as water trickles down her nose and on to her lips. Paneke pulls a flattened bottle from her lavalava and they each take a swig of fresh water. Even this is hot but the moisture soothes their dry throats.

Vents of steam obscure their path and Paneke warns Cowrie to be careful to follow her footsteps directly. Large crevices on the surface lead down to blackened depths below. It's impossible to see the bottom. Paneke bends over to pick up a lava rock and drops it into the vent. The craggy stone disappears into rising steam as the gorge eats it up. Cowrie imagines what it would be like to fall in.

The heat and steam make her dizzy. Her chest is burning. Her heart throbs. Kereru wings beat in her ears. At first it is frightening, then there is a pleasant sensation that accompanies the vibrations. But with it, a searing heat. Her hei matau burns into her chest. She grabs it. An electric current sizzles her fingertips, then her hands and travels up her right arm. It scorches her hair and her head is engulfed by flames. She lets out a piercing cry and then falls with a thud on to the hardened lava.

Paneke hears the cry and turns to see Cowrie clutching at her neck. A flame rushes up her arm and surrounds her head with a luminous halo. She drops to the ground and the fire sizzles from her hair and down a crevice. It burns into the delicate leaf of a new fern which has miraculously grown out of the split rock, leaving it brown and drooping. She rushes to Cowrie and lifts her head into her lap, pouring precious water on to her parched lips.

Paneke gently strokes her hair and calls out to Pele. After a while, Cowrie wakes to find herself strangely refreshed. She sits up. Paneke explains that Pele has tried to contact her through her bone carving. That the burning sensation was just her voice trying to be heard. It is nothing to fear. She means no harm. Cowrie is scared that her transgression in reaching for the lehua blossom is being punished. Paneke thinks this is not so, that Pele was simply trying to contact her. Cowrie is not so sure. Paneke takes the hei matau and places it on the lip of the rock crevice, near the scorched fern. She completes a protection ritual.

When she bends to pick up the bone carving, Paneke notices that the sizzled fern leaf has disappeared. It has dropped into the crevice. The fern has offered her hand for Pele's embrace. She knows they will now be safe.

Cowrie rises to her feet and is surprised to find that her body has cooled and she feels a renewed energy for the journey ahead. The vibrations have left her hei matau, made for her by Mere's brother as her farewell toanga.

It is in the shape of a fish-hook – the instrument that Maui used to pull Te ika a Maui – the North Island, out of the sea. She lets Paneke place the bone carving over her head and it rests again on her chest. This time, it is cool, soothing. She now believes the remainder of the journey will be in peace.

And so it is. They walk the twisted ocean-lava floor of Kilauea crater without drama, aside from the internal stories that the lava flows tell them with their frozen and still-steaming shapes. Near the edge of the crater, Paneke stoops to pick up a piece of crystal-clear lace that spans the distance between two rocks like a spider's web glistening in the rain. She lays the thin, translucent strands across the palm of Cowrie's hand and tells her that this is called Pele's hair and that horrendous things have happened to tourists who stole her hair from the crater rim. Later, she will take Cowrie up to the Volcano Arts Centre to show her letters from tourists who have sent back the lacy strands and pieces of rock taken from the lava fields, begging for the relics to be returned to the crater for Pele's pardon. Cowrie needs no convincing that these stories are true.

As they approach the far rim, what had seemed like dark crevices from the other side become patches of native tree-ferns and bush. They climb the lava rock and enter into the lush ferns with relief. Cowrie wants to look back to see the distance they have covered, but is afraid that, like Orpheus, she will lose her vision of Eurydice, her budding love for Koana, hovering in the space around her. She will wait until she reaches the rim of the crater before she will dare to cast back a glance.

Paneke and Cowrie spend the afternoon together exploring the Thurston lava tube then return to the Volcano Arts Centre. Cowrie is inspired by Herb Kane's paintings of Pele. One of them depicts fire smouldering in her eyes and her hair flows out from her head and down over her bare shoulders like black ropes of lava. She wears a wreath of flaming lehua blossom around her head. Her nose flares towards its base and her lips are full and luscious. She is the embodiment of fiery, creative energy. But her inherent destructiveness and power to affect others is also present. She looks proud of the fire that flames behind her eyes.

Kane calls her Pele-honua-mea, Pele of the sacred land. She is also Pele-'ai-honua, Pele the eater of land, as she gorges prey on her lava-surf down towards the waiting ocean. Her sacred spirit is Ka-'ula-o-ke-ahi, the redness of fire. The lehua blossom epitomises this scarlet rage as it thrusts its bloody spikes out from its centre. It is startlingly attractive and repellingly barbarous at once.

Cowrie senses that there is much to learn from her brush with Pele's fire. About Hawai'i, about Pele, about herself, her ancestors. She appreciates the fiery, creative energy that is an ever-present life force within her, but fears its power also. Others have been intimidated by it too. They have tried to tame it in her, douse the flames with water, restrict her wild energy. But none have succeeded.

Paneke interrupts Cowrie's broken lava thoughts and leads her into a rich ocean of sound. She emerges from Volcano House to see a large, incredibly beautiful, fiery woman standing with her bare feet apart, a wreath of scarlet lehua around her flowing, pitch-black and ashen hair. She could be Pele.

Her voice cavorts with the tunes of the 'ukulele she plucks, diving down to bass depths and then soaring up to a falsetto in one note. The echo from one blends into the other producing a sound that is guttural and heavenly at once. It is like hearing the human voice for the first time. She wonders if this erotic interplay between 'ukulele and voice is what attracted her grandfather, Apelahama, to his trade. If so, how could he ever leave this island?

Young children and adults join in the next song. They burst into a spontaneous hula and it's hard not to move with them. Everyone is laughing and singing. Paneke swings her wide hips in tune with the music. The crowd urges them on.

The wind blows the tree-ferns behind the dancers and Cowrie notices, for the first time, how similar the motion of the fern fronds is to the swinging of their hips and the dance of their fingertips. Each movement seems to describe a new story, a new sweep of the brush across canvas. Paneke beckons Cowrie to join them. Mere had taught her a poi dance, but she feels shy in the presence of these graceful bodies. A voluptuous woman gets up and joins in with her children and the audience cheers them on. Suddenly, Cowrie loses all self-consciousness and becomes a part of the motion around her. She is swept into the dance and surrenders to its seductive motion. Diane Aki's voice slides from one register to the next with amazing grace and the fingers of her musicians fly over their 'ukulele. The mamaku and smaller ferns, the scarlet 'okika flowers, the cream plumeria merge with the coloured patterns of material dancing in the wind. Cowrie imagines them all flying through the midnight-blue sky of a Chagall painting, with only the ferns connecting them to the rich, black lava of Pele.

That night, when Keo asks them how their day has

been, they fight for words and Paneke plays a tape of Aki's music while Cowrie shows Keo her new hula skills. Keo's belly jellies into motion as he joins them. Paneke fetches the lehua wreaths she has taught Cowrie to make, which they wear festively while dancing to the music. Keo breaks into a sliding falsetto. He can sing as high as Aki. He steadies on a note, then slips into a rising glissando and within a split second is singing two registers higher up the scales.

Cowrie makes him promise to teach her how to do this. It is an extraordinary sound that sends shivers of joy through her entire body.

After they work up a sweat, Paneke collapses on to the wooden verandah bench. The sun is setting over the sugar cane fields below and Cowrie thinks she might burst with happiness before she has had a chance to share this celebration of life with Mere.

There is a crash behind them. Peni and Nele burst in. Koana stands smiling in the doorway. "We see you dance hula, Cowrie," cries Nele.

Peni grins and Koana looks strangely shy. "Hope you don't mind, Cowrie," she says.

Cowrie smiles warmly. Koana breaks into a silent hula, swaying her hips to the invisible music, pretending to imitate Cowrie but doing so with a lifetime of graceful movement that she can not make awkward even when she tries.

The sun turns Koana's face orange and her fingertips become the wings of birds, each on a different flight, but in close formation with the other. Her eyes are aflame and her nostrils widen, as if to breathe in the new air needed for her inspirational dance. The sun slides down behind her and a deep orange flames up the sky. Koana is on fire. Cowrie wants to keep her flame alive until she can bear it no longer, then moisten every inch of Koana's body with her wet tongue. Koana catches her look and swings her hips out provocatively towards Cowrie, moving her body closer and closer until Cowrie wants to cry out for release.

The hula is such a sexy dance, the others do not notice the particular intensity of this energy. Koana finishes her hula and slips Cowrie a seductive smile as she tucks her lavalava back at her waist. They all clap and settle down to enjoy the evening.

After freshly roasted coffee from Kona, on the western side of the island, they exchange stories of their days. Koana tells of some Germans who arrived at the post office in search of an artist friend of theirs from East Berlin. She could not understand all of their broken English but she thinks they are looking for Eva Senkens who has been house-sitting for some Californians who shipped over a huge wine vat and rebuilt it as a home near Ka Lae. She gave them directions and they were very grateful.

Cowrie asks what kind of art the German woman does. Koana is not sure, but someone at Na'alehu said she had created a series of paintings and collages around the theme of Pele.

Keo describes the plight of one of the Portuguese cane workers who was today arrested as an overstayer without a visa or permit.

Cowrie explains this happens to Samoans, Tongans, and other Pacific Islanders in New Zealand, but a blind eye is cast towards the rich Japanese and European visitors who overstay.

Nele and Peni talk of a new Samoan boy at school who described to them the ravages of the latest hurricane that destroyed his native land.

"They come every December, just in time for Christmas," Nele adds. "Imagine having your home destroyed every Christmas."

Paneke and Cowrie describe their day, as accurately as they can. Cowrie notices that Paneke leaves out the detail of her visit from Pele so she decides not to elaborate on that.

When Cowrie gets to the bit about the 'ohi'a-lehua, Keo adds another perspective. He speaks of Ku-ka-'ohi'a-laka who is worshipped by canoe carvers because he lives inside the most-used hardwood tree, the 'ohi'a lehua. He is also the male Laka worshipped in the hula dance. At Ola'a there is an 'ohi'a lehua which is revered as the body of Laka. It will only ever bear a pair of blossoms in one season. If a branch is broken, blood will flow from the cut.

Cowrie tells them of the lone pohutukawa which is the residing place for spirits before they take leave from Te Ika a Maui at the most northern point of Aotearoa. The tree is sacred and it is tapu to violate it.

"Ah, your tapu is our kapu" ventures Keo. "That is so, that is so."

After their stories, there is a long and satisfying silence in which Cowrie meditates on the possibility of a hula dedicated from one woman dancer to another. She hopes this thought is not kapu.

Kia ora Mere,

Remember when you told me not to go into the Takatu burial ground as a kid because it was tapu? Well, it's the same here. Their 'ohi'a tree is like our pohutukawa, sacred. Paneke took me through Pele's crater, but I touched the 'ohi'a blossom (lehua) en route and Pele reminded me of her power by setting my hei matau on fire. It scorched my skin but the bone carving remained intact. A warning? (Don't tell anyone back home I transgressed. It might call up some mean spirits there). But despite this, I'm so glad you encouraged me to come. Keo showed me a photo of my grandfather. He's not fat and luscious (like me!) but tall and strong. Yet I have his eyes! Hope you got the cowrie shell I sent. Dark brown with cream markings. Bi-cultural too eh? Haha! How's the new marae progressing? I know you can't go in while it's being built – but are you doing some of the tukutuku panels? I'd like to be back for the opening ceremony, yet still need to explore further here. How long will it be? Another 6 months?

Say hi to Matiu and Maata from me – and Wiremu if he's back from Oz yet.

Cowrie.

Nele and Peni have a week off school for mid-term break. Aka usually takes them but he has gone fishing with a friend. Koana can only change her post office shift for two days so Cowrie offers to take the kids over to Puako with her, and Koana will join them at the end of the week. Puako is on the western side of the island and Cowrie has been asked to house-sit and feed the cats by a friend of Koana's. She accepted willingly, looking forward to exploring the island further and is relieved to be able to give Koana a break and return some of her hospitality beyond just a rent cheque.

As the holiday draws nearer, Nele and Peni become more and more excited. They practise by sleeping out on the back porch with Cowrie, wrapped up in blankets pulled around them like sleeping bags. Cowrie thinks it amusing, since it's too hot for a sleeping bag here, even at night. Within half an hour, they are lying snoring, arms flung out to their sides, blankets drooping off the edge of the verandah.

Finally, Monday arrives. Peni and Nele load up Honu with beer crates and cardboard boxes of their favourite possessions, some fishing nets, lines, their 'ukulele and as much food as they can lay their hands on. Their idea of essential supplies relies mainly on three weeks' allowance spent on cans of coke and endless packets of kalo chips – labelled taro and sliced thin for the US market. Cowrie is tempted to dump the coke overboard. Mere always used to call it "gut rot – the price of colonialism" and told Cowrie to get used to the sweet taste of fresh rainwater they collected in the tank. She had. But she could hardly dump the coke without chucking the kalo chips and Cowrie has to admit she loves them. So she decides to give in. They'll be begging for fresh fish after a few days.

After much drama packing the truck and tying down everything then having to redo it to make seats for Peni and Nele, who have decided to travel in the back after all, Cowrie toots the horn and Koana comes out to farewell them. She lifts Peni on to the tray and tells him to look after Nele, kissing him and tickling his belly. Then she does the same with Nele. Through the rear-vision mirror, Cowrie notices that they are openly warm and sad to leave her. She wants to jump out and be held in Koana's arms also but she dares not get too close. Ever since Koana's hula touched her hips, she has felt electric anywhere near her friend. She doesn't want to frighten her away and yet she suspects there might be a flicker of attraction from Koana also. It's so hard to know how to share these feelings.

While Cowrie muses over this, Koana has walked around the back of Honu and now she lays her arm over Cowrie's, which rests on the window ledge. Cowrie is startled. Koana grins. Her large brown eyes glisten like macadamias hanging from the trees in the afternoon rain. Cowrie looks down at her feet. She can meet this gaze no longer. Koana touches her cheek lightly with her forefinger and says, "Now you take gentle care of my kamali'i, Cowrie." Before Cowrie can answer, she kisses her on her left cheek and whispers, "Take care of yourself also. I will miss you. I come in a few days."

The kiss leaves a moist dot beside her lips. Cowrie could have sworn it was Koana's tongue on her cheek. The flames in her body rise up to meet the wet kiss like Pele's lava sizzling into the moist ocean. She tries hard to keep cool.

"No worries, Koana. We'll have a ball," she says, glancing back at the twins. Both their noses are pressed up against the window behind her and they are grinning gleefully. For a moment, Cowrie thinks they can see right through her, then realises they are just overjoyed to be starting out on a new adventure. Relieved, she touches Koana's hand reassuringly. Koana's fingers wrap around her own and Cowrie blushes. Koana releases her hand and Cowrie lets off the brake and throttles into gear. Looking into the rear-vision mirror, she sees Koana surrounded by a halo of dust. As it settles, she emerges like an angel from a dark rain cloud and then shrinks until all Cowrie can pick out is a mound in the distance. She longs to return and embrace this woman fully. She drives on.

As they pass the turn-off to Ka Lae, she thinks of the fisherman's tale of the rebuilding of the sacred heiau on the forbidden island: the nuclear testing site. Anger swells within her as she remembers the struggle for Ngati Whatua to reclaim their land at Bastion Point, Aotearoa. After months of occupation, five hundred police were sent in to arrest two hundred Ngati Whatua and their supporters. They'd trained for this moment and each person resisted peacefully, dropping limply in the arms of struggling policemen – some of them Maori. Cowrie never forgot the sight of one young Ngati Whatua woman looking into the eyes of a Maori policeman and challenging his betrayal of their cause. Moments like these were etched on her brain forever. They spoke more than all the rhetoric ever could. They were like markings in the sand – a trail of survival and change – recording all the betrayals and broken promises along the way. And they were never simple. One tribe pitched against the other, each trying to survive within an alien system of possession which marked out land as an object rather than a living part of the spirit.

How could anyone presume to own land? A Navajo poet who stayed with Cowrie over the Women Writers' Hui explained that her people did not believe in land ownership, that we are all only caretakers of the land. "The land belongs to she who takes care of it," she'd said.

Cowrie believed it too. She looks over towards the rocky cliffs of Ka Lae and wonders how the Maori waka ever launched there. She feels a sudden chill shudder down her spine, resting itself at the base of her backbone. A strange sensation of waiting for something to happen.

She decides to stop for a break and bring the kids inside the cab for a while. She pulls over and slides out of her seat. The chilling feeling does not leave her until long after they have had refreshments and are back on the road west.

At Kona, they stop for lunch. Kalo soaked in coconut milk and wrapped in banana leaves. Followed by Nele's first batch of kalo chips! Koana has prepared a feast for them in the basket she gave the twins to look after. Fresh mangoes and bananas and some raw 'ahi drenched in lime juice. Cowrie licks her fingers after the feed and wishes Koana were here so she could work her tongue between each of her fingers in turn, drinking in the coconut and lime and the sweet skin salt. Instead, she settles for wiping the sticky substance from Nele's cheeks with the edge of her lavalava while Peni pushes his face into the sand to see how much he can pick up with the juice acting as a glue.

The beach is filled with people, including tourists who usually just drive through Na'alehu. Cowrie is not keen to stay, but the kids are excited by it all. They check out a few shops by the sea, and Nele is overjoyed when she finds Hilo Hattie's. It is filled to the brim with all kinds of hats, from woven island hats, like flax ones back home, with brightly painted bands, to bowlers and top hats. Nele fancies a black bowler hat and swaggers down the shop with it on. The Hawai'ian youth who serves them enjoys Nele's performance. Getting jealous, Peni tries on a grey top hat. Cowrie's hard-earned cash is getting low. She will need to find work soon or return home, but she cannot resist the twins.

When they emerge from the shop, decked out in their new hats, Peni and Nele take on new personae. They hold their heads high and walk like haole, in long, exaggerated strides mimicking the corporate business men they have seen on the television. Cowrie wishes Koana could see them now. Even on the beach, they keep their colonial hats perched on their ragged mops of hair. Peni picks up a twig and pretends to smoke it. As they sit on a rock, looking out to sea, Cowrie is reminded of the old Goldie paintings of early Maoris after European settlement. Mere had one of an old man with a bowler hat on and a pounamu earring dangling from one ear. Another was of a Maori woman with a beautiful moko and a child slung on her back. Both of their faces looked sad in the paintings. Were they? Or was this just the European portrayal of them? Even Peni and Nele are uncharacteristically quiet and, for a moment, frozen in time.

The road north continues to follow the coast and soon they come across an old art deco style building painted cream with coffee-brown features. Across the sloping semi-round roof is a sign marking the Aloha Theatre. Cowrie is amused to see the English spelling of theatre on the top, just below the crown which sets the building's date as 1932 and the American spelling below on a swinging sign which reads 'Aloha Theater'. She points out the difference to Nele, who loves playing with words. Nele notices that the cafe is also with the modern spelling and after much pleading from her companions, and a thirsty glance at the expresso sign, Cowrie hauls Honu to a stop a little further on and they walk back to the building, past the Aloha Village Store which is stacked with luscious-looking natural foods. The kids stock up on sesame and apricot bars while Cowrie fills her kete with fresh fruit and unsalted macadamia nuts, dried papaya and different samples of local kai moana.

From Kainaliu, the road forks left up to Kailua Bay and from there up to Kiholo Bay. Evidence of lava-flows from Mauna Loa can be seen spanning both sides of the road: an alien moonscape with patches of lush green palms from time to time near the ocean.

Honu rattles into Puako on a dusty road and Peni reads the scrumpled-up map which Patsy had scrawled on the back of a cheque. Her house is on a dirt road parallel with the beach and as they turn into the drive, three mangy cats appear from beneath the cottage. By the time they draw up level with the house, the cats have disappeared in a screen of dust.

The ground appears to be a very fine sand over rock and behind the house, in front of the truck, is a welcoming pond. Nele and Peni rush over to it and are delighted to see large fish splashing about. Cowrie is amazed. A natural brackish pond with fat trout by the dozen. This is too good to be true. She asks the kids if these fish are edible. They shake their heads. They're not sure. Cowrie resolves to do a bit of netting after they've unpacked.

There are dust screens on all the doors and windows, for good reason. The cottage is open plan with mattresses on the floor. Cowrie slings her hammock up on the side porch behind the mosquito netting. Nele and Peni each dive for their chosen beds and the unpacking ritual begins.

After they've emptied the truck, Cowrie and Nele unwrap Koana's raw marinated 'ahi for dinner and each of them sets to making their favourite salads with the sparse vegies available on the island. The heat turns lettuce to cooked cabbage so Cowrie chooses fresh tomato and basil sliced with green peppers and Nele stands on a stool to grate carrot into a bowl of orange and coconut juice.

Suddenly, there is an ungodly scream outside. Cowrie rushes through the screen door, letting it slam against the house and is horrified to see Peni lying on his back on the rocks beside the pool, gashes in his foot and blood everywhere.

Fucking wildcats, thinks Cowrie, but they are not to be seen. Instead, the fish in the pool are crashing themselves against the side in an effort to reach the blood-oozing foot. They flap wildly against each other, one jumping into the air and landing high and dry before it slithers, snake-like, back into the water.

Peni's screams and waving arms have died down to foot-clutching moans. Cowrie bends to inspect the damage. A series of cuts line the soft flesh under his arch and his eyes have the look of one who has seen a terrible sight but can still hardly believe it. Maybe this was the chilling premonition I had while driving past Ka Lae, thinks Cowrie, hugging his foot to her breast as she wraps her lavalava around it to bandage the wound and allow him to hobble back indoors, while Nele holds his hand.

After she has dressed the wounds properly and applied her herbal remedies, Cowrie asks the twins if there is an Hawai'ian version of piranha. They have both seen fish that eat human flesh on television but they do not know of any such fish in waters around the island. Cowrie has no idea what led these fish to their frenzy but from her knowledge of sea creatures she understands that their behaviour is most unusual.

That night, Cowrie lets them turn on the old black and white tv in the corner. The only picture they can get is a rerun of *Out on a Limb*. The kids think Shirley MacLaine is hilarious and they cover their heads with towels and pretend to see stories in a large, round piece of lava rock which they mount on a spoon. The spoon conducts magical energy which allows them to be anything they like. Soon they are so lost in their own games, they forget about the television. Cowrie flicks it off with the dusty remote and heaves a sigh of relief as they gradually drift into sleep. She buries her nose back into a book on Hawai'i she has picked off the shelf. *Pele*, by Herb Kane.

Tena koe Kuini,

Mahalo for your letter. It arrived just before
I left for Puako and I only opened it tonight.
Glad to hear the writing hui plans are going
well. Nele and Peni, (Koana's twins) are now
asleep and it's hauntingly quiet, except for the
ocean. I brought the kids over to house-sit an
old cottage by the sea. Koana will join us at
end of week. Can't wait! Hey — ask Keri if she
knows of any fish like piranha in Hawai'i?
Sounds bizarre, but pond fish attacked Peni's
foot today. Went into frenzy when blood
appeared. Weird.

Reading a fascinating book about Pele by Herb
Kane — local Hawai'ian artist of great mana.
Stunning paintings. Pele embodies spiritual
power of the land here, just like Robin
Kahukiwa's depictions of Papatuanuku back
home. Home? Well, Hawai'i is starting to feel
like home as well.

Have been dreaming about Koana. I think she
likes me but she's definitely not a dyke — yet!
Can't imagine her changing. Very traditional

family values. Then again, you overcame that, eh? (am writing on aero not p.c. so Raglan P.O. don't read it all first!)

Enjoying Nele and Peni. Interesting mixture of US colonialism and traditional Hawai'ian values. Koana has worked hard to preserve latter. Good on her. Koana . . . How can I stop thinking of her? Should I just accept our friendship or dare I imagine more? We've talked around it vaguely. She's questioned her life with Aka and doesn't want a new heterosexual partner at present. But I sense she's not ready to imagine the possibility of loving a woman fully. I want to respect her needs but not repress my own. The endless dilemma. It's like being a teenager again – feeling the attraction from both sides but being too afraid to act on it. Maybe I should be a neuter after all? Celibacy certainly has its attractions! I'm beginning to feel creative again, writing and sketching. What's the latest on the writers' hui?

Miss you heaps.

Arohanui – Cowrie XXX.

Peni perches on the edge of a lava shelf at Puako beach while Cowrie and Nele try to convince him to dangle his foot into the healing salt waters of the ocean. He is not keen on introducing his wounds to shark-infested seas. "The shark is Pele's brother," Nele says. "Remember, we learned that in school last term. Ka-moho-ali'i. When he's not in the water, he lives in human form on the northern edge of the crater. Even Pele is scared of him. But she'll make sure you're protected."

Cowrie remembers reading something about this up at Volcano House. He was the shark god and Pele's family offered him their corpses to become sharks and act as protectors of the family. All over Hawai'i the shark spirit protected those who respected its powers. At the time, she thought of the Tongan fella, Seketoa, who used to play cricket with them at varsity. It was when a shark attack on a small boy at St Clair's Beach in Dunedin made headlines. He told her that he was named after a fella who turned himself into a shark to escape death from his jealous, older brother. That shark now protects the whole family. He didn't believe sharks would attack without some kind of reason. Cowrie wonders what Seke would've thought about the flesh-gashing fish in Patsy's pond.

By now, Nele has convinced Peni to gingerly place one toe, then the next until his whole foot is submerged in the water. At first it stings and he yells out bitterly. But gradually, the water begins to soothe his cuts. Peni has calmed down considerably when suddenly he rips his foot out of the water. Nele leans over to get a better look.

"It's just 'opae, Peni. See, they want to tickle your toes." Nele reaches her hand down into the sea and half a dozen large shrimps migrate to her fingertips, their feet dangling down and brushing against her skin. Peni carefully places his foot back into the water. The shrimps nuzzle up and when he wriggles his toes, they swim away, only to return to see what they've missed.

Cowrie checks he's all right then walks back up the rocks to get the ripped cloth lavalava which she's been using to bandage his foot. She bends down to reach it and rising back to her full height she notices a fin out on the horizon. It moves rapidly through the waves towards them, then veers to the left. Peni and Nele are oblivious, now deep into stories of sea monsters and how Popeye fought the giant octopus. Cowrie keeps a wary eye on the large fish. It moves back and forth along the reef, at some distance from them, as if guarding something.

Nele helps her dry and bandage Peni's foot, pretending to be a shrimp as she dives in and out of Peni's toes, making him giggle and protest at once. Once the cloth is carefully wound back around Peni's foot, he hobbles up the rock shelf with them. Cowrie glances back out to sea. The shark has disappeared as quickly as it came. There is no sign of it, even on the far horizon. She wonders if she imagined its presence.

Further along the lava shelf, Peni complains that his bandage is coming off. Cowrie bends down to tie it tighter and notices strange patterns in the rocks. "Some artistic people have been here. Look at this," she exclaims, pointing to some stick figures of people running and others holding paddles above their heads.

Nele kneels down for a closer look. "Ki'i pohaku," she says.

Cowrie waits for an explanation.

Peni prods her. "You know, rock drawings."

Nele adds, for good measure, "They are called petroglyphs, silly," and Peni pokes her in the ribs for showing

42

him up.

Cowrie knew the good behaviour had to come to a halt sometime. She attempts a diversion. "Ok, you lot. Tell me about them. I know nothing, except for some rock drawings I've seen back home. They were mostly of taniwha and animals."

"What's taniwha?" asks Peni.

"Mythical creatures. Monsters. Usually found in water," replies Cowrie, glad she has avoided a confrontation between them.

By now all three are on their hands and knees, bent down over the rocks, examining the drawings. Some have almost faded away with the action of the sea water. Cowrie asks them how old these sculptures are. The twins are unsure, but they know it's several hundred years since they were done. "Before haole arrived," adds Peni, authoritatively. So they are pagan symbols, thinks Cowrie. She looks more closely at the figures before her. They bear strange and fascinating head gear. It seems as if spirits are issuing out from the tops of their heads.

"Mum says there's heaps of these drawings on a trail inland from the beach," pipes up Nele. "She said to tell you to check them out. I forgot until now."

Peni yells out that this one with spiked hair looks like a punk. The figure has a huge, barbed head-dress.

After musing over the artwork, they walk back on the other side of the road and there is a hand-painted sign sticking out of the lava rock marked "Kaeo trail, ½ mile. Petr . . ." The sign is broken but the arrow below the word Kaeo points inland. That'll be Koana's trail, thinks Cowrie. She longs to follow it but knows she must wait for Peni's foot to heal. Half a mile could be a long way to hobble.

"Let's go see the pictures," pleads Peni.

"But what about your foot?"

"No worries. See. It's getting better," he claims, placing all his weight on it and walking with only a slight limp.

"Perhaps we'll go when Koana comes."

"Come on Cowrie. Let's go now," urges Nele.

"That's not far. We walk further than that every day."

"Yeah," agrees Peni.

Cowrie pauses for a moment. She's not in the mood to carry back a wounded soldier, even if he's asserting bravery now. But her curiosity gets the better of her and she agrees. The three of them follow the track which is marked with small piles of stones every few hundred feet. Scrawny trees struggle to grow out of the hardened magma and provide welcome relief from the hot sun. The pace is all right for Peni. It's slow going, moving among the volcanic rock, and it is vital to watch where the feet fall lest they slip down a crack. Cowrie thinks of the journey through the Kilauea crater with Paneke and is relieved that the sign marks this as only half a mile away.

Only a few hundred feet inland, Nele points out some marks on the rock. Large, rounded mounds of lava are etched with lines of stick figures that look like giant, moving ladders. The figures are poised in challenge mode. They are either marching or stalking each other with legs and arms outstretched.

The line of figures seems to mark some kind of trail and reminds Cowrie of the curious markings that delineate topographical maps and ancient religious sites in early Aboriginal drawings. From standing height they resemble a large insect, a centipede perhaps.

They enter an area of more

dense bush scattered amongst the rocks. The scraggy trees seem to grow where little water is needed. This landscape resembles Rangitoto Island. It's hard to believe that vegetation has a chance of growing out of this lava rock. Rangitoto is also volcanic and yet large pohutukawa, like the 'ohi'a trees, manage to spread their waving arms out of the hardened lava and drop their blood-red stamens on to the black basalt rocks below.

A couple of times, they lose the trail, but instinct leads them back to the most worn path. It is difficult to get bearings when there is so much lava around them and little vegetation. Every now and again, a lizard emerges from a crack or lies still, sunning its back on a rock, hoping no one will spy its presence. Sweat is pouring down all three of them. The midday heat is unbearable and they hop from rock to rock and pause every now and again under a tree for some relief. Cowrie regrets that she did not insist that they return home for lunch and refreshments. Had they planned the trip, they would have brought plenty of liquid. She sometimes forgets the power of the heat to dehydrate the body on this island. Peni and Nele seem to be able to stand it better, but even they are complaining they have not brought their coke with them.

However, the fascination of discovering the rock drawings as they come across more symbols and figures carries them on until they reach a large clearing comprising giant mounds of softly curving lava separated by cracks and a few loose stones. Each is like the body of a large woman sleeping, her pregnant belly bared to the sun. Standing on the edge of this ancient site, Cowrie is overwhelmed by its cracked magnificence.

She contemplates etchings on a nearby dome. At first, it is difficult to distinguish the shapes from the natural rock lines. Gradually, she picks out figures that seem to delineate family groups. The men appear to have muscular, triangular bodies.

Other figures are suspended in mid air. One holds an object like a turtle by its fin. Another swings a gourd.

Cowrie is pleased to find some female figures that describe large body shapes rather than just the stick figures of modern anorexia. Some look as if they are about to burst into flight, soar off the rocks and into space. Feet poised, arms outstretched. One depicts the luscious rounded shape of an ancient fertility goddess. The woman holds herself proudly, her rounded breasts erect and her head facing the sculptor. Her arms swing out from her shoulders and a curious kind of halo surrounds her head. It emerges from behind her shoulders and forms a perfect circle shimmering out from her brain.

Nele and Peni have found some runners on a nearby rock. Cowrie weaves her way between the belly formations to join them. Peni thinks they are hilarious. One looks demented as he runs with the arms and legs of a chicken.

Below it are figures with paddle-like shapes raised above their heads. They stand in threatening poses.

"Why do they hold their paddles above their heads?" asks Nele.

"To keep them dry, moron," answers Peni.

Nele glares at him. "They look like taiaha, as if they are participating in a ritual challenge or war dance," offers Cowrie.

They stare at her as if she is mad. "Ok. Taiaha are pointed spears. They are wooden, like canoe paddles, and are used in ceremonial Maori dances and challenges."

"Are they used to kill people?" asks Peni, eyes alight.

"I'm not sure if they were used as weapons in that sense."

"So, d'ya reckon these warriors are challenging each other?"

"Well, they could be. I can't see why else they would

carry their paddles so high and adopt such a threatening pose," explains Cowrie, "but I can't be sure."

So many unexplained stories in these rocks, fascinating details of past lives. Cowrie is high from the inspiration they give her, the heat that shimmers off the black rocks like the desert at midday. She feels slightly giddy with a buzzing at the back of her brain.

She glances over her shoulder to spy a bird-like figure crouched on a rock. It seems to move, but is solidly etched into the lava. On closer inspection, it looks more like a stylised dragonfly, with two smaller oval egg shapes accompanying its solo flight.

Other similar figures have trailers dangling from their arms or wings. Cowrie cannot take her eyes off them. They seem to be more like gods or symbols than the other stick figures.

Nele has pounced on her favourite images: animals. She has found some that look like dogs or pigs with curly tails and stylised ones that are like chickens or birds in flight. But best of all is a huge, fat turtle that appears to be swimming over the top of a breast-like mound.

Cowrie's mind blurs. She tries to focus on the turtle, but every time it swims away from her. She lies face down on the curved surface as a huge wave rolls towards her. She re-enters the dream. Her heart pounds and her breathing quickens with fear. The wave is about to engulf her, but suddenly she is flying with its motion rather than fighting against it. She soars through the air with the wave on her tail, then turns around and faces into its concave hollow. It is dark.

When she opens her eyes again, two large, hazel pupils stare into her own. "Koana, Koana," she moans. But it is not Koana. It is Nele, alarmed that Cowrie fainted on the rock, and she is holding Cowrie's head in the palms of her hands. Nele looks so like Koana that Cowrie is comforted, relaxed. Peni appears out of the corner of her vision, a kumara-shaped root in his hand. With a sharp rock he makes an incision along its belly and holds it above Cowrie's lips, dripping a sweet–sour moisture on to her tongue. He breaks open another root and shares it with Nele.

When Cowrie has regained enough strength, she crawls into the shade, arms outstretched, and Nele and Peni nap at her side. From above, they look like the dragonfly shape etched into the rock: Cowrie with wings spread out and each of the twins curled up in foetal position on either side of her, like oval eggs, sleeping before they are fully hatched.

At dusk, when it is cooler, the triad make their way back over the hardened lava rock, following the trail carefully. Finally, they return to the Puako road and are relieved to reach their dusty haven to be greeted by Patsy's scrawny cats screeching for their dinner.

While throwing together a salad, Cowrie is mortified that she took children out on a trail in the midday heat without even thinking of taking liquid with her. The return journey was only marked as a mile from the road but she figures they covered at least three miles meandering. No problem to walk three miles without liquid back home, but here it could be fatal.

She is disturbed that the exhaustion and heat brought back her childhood nightmare but elated that she did not end up crushed on the rocks by the tidal wave. The last shape she remembered before losing consciousness was the turtle.

She fingers Apelahama's coconut-shell turtle which she wears around her neck next to her hei matau, wondering, as she did with the shark, if it is a harmful or a protective spirit.

Kia ora Mere,

Thanks for the letter. Koana forwarded it to the beach cottage I'm sharing with Nele and Peni at Puako (east side of the big island). Sorry to hear you're not feeling well. What does Aunty Rawinia say? She knows more than the Pakeha doctors. I'd check with her also.

Today Nele and Peni took me out on the Kaeo Trail to the site of some ancient Hawai'ian rock carvings. Can't get over the similarity to those South Island caves you took me to. Like at home, they're all pre-Pakeha images. Fascinating. Canoes, wild chickens, elongated dogs that look like aardvarks, a hula dancer juggling gourds (one of my favourites) – a whole world of talkstory etched into lava rock. Even a turtle: remember my childhood recurring dream? I've had strange turtle experiences since arriving: first the dream again, then a giant turtle on the road to Keo's, one etched into the coconut bowl I ate from, and in the heat today I collapsed back into the dream. Turtle woman is a strong figure here, like Pele. Maybe she's trying to tell me something?

I knew they'd choose you to direct the tukutuku panel-weaving for the new marae. Great! I can't wait to see them. Is Moana involved in the carving?

How's that new fella in the store coping now? If he didn't know whether the fish he was cooking was hoki or kahawai, he won't last long! Tell Moana to sell him shark fillets and call them "lemon dory". You'd make enough profit to come visit me here! Kuini told me about a Tainui fella who ordered fish and chips at Raglan from a Pakeha joker. He paid for the chips and said, "The fish is ours by treaty, but thanks for cooking it up." Then he sauntered off. The owner was too stunned to follow! Cheeky, eh? But historically correct!

The twins are scrapping. I'd better see to it. You'd love them, the little buggers!

Give yourself a big hug from me – and try some of that herbal mixture in my top drawer. It really works. Better than drugs. Aunty Rawinia has more if you like it.

Arohanui – Cowrie XX.

The next few days are spent swimming and exploring the Kawaihae Coast. The twins had begun the usual bickering when kids run out of new ideas and get bored with each other's company. Cowrie's next tactic, after unwittingly exhausting them, and herself, on the Kaeo Trail in the midday heat, is to begin the day with unlimited body-surfing on the beach of their choice where they can spend time with other kids until joyful tiredness sets in. By late afternoon, they are begging to go home, where they sleep in her hammock until dinner, usually around dusk. This allows her time alone to rest and read and catch up on her sketches and journal entries. Sitting under the palms at the beach, she does most of her reading, then writes when they return home.

Today, Nele and Peni decide to see if the dried-out palm bowls fallen from the base of the branches can be used as makeshift surfboards. What they lack in buoyancy, they make up for in gaining attention from the other kids, and soon they are all gathering up the flattened bowls and taking them for a swim. One enterprising youth tries one as a skim-board over the calmer water and soon the new rage takes on. Peni's foot seems to have miraculously recovered, enough to give this novel activity a go. Nele makes friends with some local girls from Kona. For them, Nele's home at Na'alehu, on the other coast of their island, is worlds away.

Later that day, ploughing through Patsy's books, Cowrie discovers more about the petroglyphs. The strange dragonfly figure is a Lono symbol. The vertical body and wing-like arms describe the wooden image of Lono, the God carried during tax collecting and celebrated in the Makahiki festival which followed the event. According to Malo's description written in 1835, the Makahiki idol was a stick of wood with a figure-head at the end, and a cross-piece (kea) tied to the neck, from which feather lei hung. By the time the Makahiki God arrived, the konohiki had collected taxes and presented them as offerings to the gods. In the resulting ceremony, the land was now considered free from tabu. When the image was carried forward to the next place, its face looked backwards.

Cowrie imagines the ancient ceremony in reverse. Maybe if locals put tapu back on their land, it would prevent the collecting of rates and the land would revert to its original inhabitants. In her mind, she creates a unique version of the Makahiki idol. Its body is that of a large wahine toa and the cross-piece is a broom handle carved from manuka. Dangling from each end are flax kete for the gathering of land taxes. The carved figure-head is that of Hinekaro, who will exact utu on those who ignore her pleas. There is a festival of celebration after the gathering of taxes attended by all to decide on the distribution of the wealth. After rates are returned to the elders, the remainder goes to the kuia for the education and health of the children and old people. Cowrie smiles. She knows that this thought will find its way over the seas to Hinekaro, as sure as the waka left Ka Lae for Aotearoa. The rest is up to her.

While Malo's words make some sense, Cowrie does not believe all that she reads. The challenging pose of the figures with canoe paddles raised above their heads, which is strikingly similar to that of the Maori challenge using the taiaha raised above the head and vigorous tongue-flicking reminiscent of a tuatara to warn the intruders that they mean business, is described as being insignificant by some academics. She sketches the figures on the page, then rereads their words.

"The many pictures of men holding canoe paddles horizontally over the head are probably mere symbols for paddlers. The position shown is of no importance in itself."

Clearly, these academics had never seen a Maori challenge. Cowrie cannot get these figures out of her mind. They remind her of home. She has no way of knowing, but she trusts her instinct. Many of the books play down the importance of the drawings etched into the rocks just as the first missionaries tried to destroy these apparently pagan gods of the early Hawai'ians. But Cowrie knows they are still alive, still active. Pele's angry outbursts of volcanic rage are living proof.

The canoe men with their raised paddles also remind her of rock drawings she'd seen at the Opihi River site back home. In one, the canoe prow almost formed a perfect wave over the front of the waka and the standing figures appeared to be poling the river, legs apart and poles raised. It's a while since Cowrie has seen them but they bear a strange relationship to the Hawai'ian figures which she can not ignore.

Cowrie considers herself lucky to have been sent to look after three mangy cats in a dusty Puako cottage with pet piranha in the garden pond, if only to have discovered for herself these glimpses of ancient Hawai'i, as well as having an excuse to act up with the kids and allow Koana some much needed space from them.

Koana. Delicious Koana. Those inviting eyes. Those luscious, ample hips that move with such grace. She wonders if Tutu Kini, Koana's grandmother, was as beautiful and managed to work such charms on her grandfather, Apelahama. There must have been a very special connection between them for him to have kept her address, the fragment of coconut shell and the photos. The photos! Perhaps Kini is in one of them? They are all of family groups. Keo's father is there. But surely Keo would have said if Koana's grandmother was present? She must ask him. Or Koana.

She hears Nele and Peni whispering. That means they are about to swing out of the hammock and arrive in the kitchen with extraordinary hunger pangs, as if they have not eaten all day. She packs away her books and opens the fridge door. It is alarmingly empty.

Peni appears in the doorway. "What's for dinner, oops, tea, Cowrie?"

Cowrie wrinkles her brow and rubs her chin. "What about raw Puako ika with marinated korokoro?" she answers.

"What's that?" grimaces Peni.

"Puako Piranha with marinated toes. Yours!" laughs Cowrie.

They settle for bananas rolled in lime juice and grated coconut, baked soft.

Cowrie did contemplate netting one of the pond fish as an act of utu for that part of Peni's foot it gashed. But she thinks the better of it. For all she knows, these brackish pond piranha could be guardian spirits for some Hawai'ian family. She does not fancy being turned into a blood-frenzied fish and ending up in somebody's back yard.

Chomp! Chomp! Chomp! Cowrie opens one eye groggily to see Nele in the kitchen, perched on her stool, chopping fruit for breakfast with the huge machete grasped awkwardly in her hand. Chomp, chomp. Cowrie swings out of her hammock and is by her side in an instant. Nele grins, proud of her efforts. Cowrie hesitates a moment. She must not grab the machete away as her instinct tells her to do. "Fine, Nele. I love fresh fruit salad for breakfast. But remember I said not to use the machete without me being here?"

"But you are here, Cowrie."

"Ok, Nele, you know what I mean. I need to be beside you. Tell ya what, I'll show you how to hold it properly. You never know, you may need it one day. But it'll be difficult because your hands are still small. See. Watch this." Cowrie demonstrates the safe way to use the instrument.

Peni smells the attraction of potential conflict and food at once and is beside them, hair standing up from his head as if he's been plugged into Freddie Mercury tapes all night. Nele thinks he looks like the rock figures they'd seen carved into the lava at the beach, with their spiky headdress. Peni does not seem impressed. He's more interested in the machete being wielded with skill in front of his still-bleary eyes.

After a while, the fascination of being able to use a once-forbidden tool wears off and is replaced by the dawning awareness that Koana arrives today. She is coming on the bus that circles the island and Cowrie promised Honu would be waiting at the junction of Route 19 and Puako Road, packed with smiling faces. The twins decide to make a lei to welcome her. Cowrie wonders where they will find flowers in this dusty landscape but they return from the bush with large glossy green leaves and make a head lei. Their excitement is infectious. Cowrie realises she is buzzing too.

The old bus grinds to a halt in dust which clears to reveal two people, Koana and a rather ragged-looking fellow with tobacco-stained fingers. Koana tells them he is going to visit his nephew at Puako Beach and can they give him a ride?

"No worries," says Cowrie, indicating that he should jump up on to the tray if he wants a lift. She is slightly annoyed that he has taken the edge off seeing Koana, just with family present.

Koana greets the twins with love. Peni climbs up into the tray with the nicotine man and Nele joins Cowrie and Koana in the cab. Koana seems pleased to see her but not as pleased as Cowrie would've liked. She has been aching to touch her, to brush softly against her cheek in greeting. Instead, Koana smiles widely and says, "Mahalo, Cowrie," to thank her for looking after the twins then edges into the cab, Nele tucking into her soft folds of charcoal belly. Cowrie glances sideways at them. She smiles. What she would give to be Nele right now, eh? She lets go of her expectations. They are fantasy. Koana's family have adopted her as whanau. Isn't that enough?

When they arrive back at Puako, Cowrie fixes lunch while the twins tell Koana of their adventures. Peni takes her out to see the 'piranhas'. Koana does not know what fish they are either. They recall the bodysurfing, the food, the other kids, the Kaeo trail, how they rescued Cowrie when she fainted. Cowrie concentrates on the preparation of kai. She hopes Koana will not realise how she'd stupidly put them all at risk by not insisting on taking juice on the walk. Koana listens intently to every detail.

They talk in Ka'u Hawai'ian and Cowrie can only pick up the drift of a few sentences. But it sounds like the kids have had a good time and that's her main concern.

Later that night, after the twins have gone to bed, finally exhausted, Koana sits on the porch sipping tea with Cowrie.

"Mahalo, my friend. You have treated my kamali'i well. They adore you." Cowrie blushes.

"They're great kids, Koana. They're independent and know how to amuse themselves. I enjoy them."

"'Ae. They've had to fend for themselves since their makua left. But Aka's been ok too. He's taken them for weekends and holidays. It's not easy bringing up kids on your own, but they seem to learn more from it. Let's hope they make better relationships themselves, eh?"

"Yeah."

"You ever been married, Cowrie?"

Cowrie has been dreading the question. "Yep. We were together five years. Raised a son from my partner's former relationship. Choice kid actually. He still comes to visit me up North in the holidays."

"Do you see him often?"

"The kid? Once a year."

"No, your husband."

Cowrie takes in a deep breath. Why does this always have to be such a big deal? Every social occasion, at the workplace, everywhere people gather together, social welfare forms, census, all government departments. Always, it feels like covering up. And they say it's no big deal these days. But it still wears you down, having to explain all the time. Or not explain and feel left out.

"Well, he's a she actually. I was in a relationship with a woman and we raised a child from her former marriage." Cowrie pauses.

Koana is silent. She remains looking down at her feet. Finally she says, "That's a shame, Cowrie. Every woman deserves the love of a good man."

Cowrie is furious. If this wasn't Koana she'd walk out. Or argue. But she cares about this friend and wants her to understand. So, every woman deserves the love of a good man? Like Aka, who left? Like Koana's uncle, who abused her own kids, like Cowrie's stepfather, who tried to touch her and had his hand bitten by her in self-defence?

Koana sits quietly for a long time afterwards. Cowrie decides to call it a day and excuses herself. She goes for a long walk down to the lava-rock beach and curses the oceans for allowing such beautiful feelings to be turned into ugliness through ignorance.

She must figure out a way to be able to communicate feelings to Koana so that she understands better. Of course, it's a lot easier to do with a relative stranger. But Cowrie doesn't care what the general public thinks any more. She does care that those around her understand and accept her as she accepts them. The problem here is that het women always think you're going to hit up on them, like men do. And this is seldom true. Cowrie had been lulled into a false sense of security. She'd felt so at home with Koana, like a sister. And she also feels attracted to her. Here lies the problem. How to communicate this experience, the sense of alienation and not seem like a threat to the other person.

Cowrie thinks back to her childhood, how often she'd sat at the edge of the Pacific Ocean and wished she could dive in, be carried away by a dolphin or tortoise to a land that was more accepting, more loving. But there were no tortoises off the coast of Aotearoa and maybe there was no such land either. Sometimes she'd wished to be carried into the deep, black waters. To feel the relief of their wet darkness embracing her, taking her to their depths where she could be released from this agony. Sometimes the water would ripple as a fish swam by and Cowrie would then think her wishes had been answered and feel strangely relieved. After several hours of midnight meditation on the rocks, she'd walk home and slink into bed, unnoticed.

Mere would never ask where she'd been. She always had the feeling Mere knew, and accepted.

When Cowrie returns to the cottage, she is relieved to find Koana asleep on the woven matting, Nele and Peni curled up around her. She creeps out to the porch with a candle and her notebook and writes until she feels ok again. Between the writing and the sea, she always manages to survive.

The night is hot and sticky. Cowrie drifts in and out of nightmares. The giant wave that haunted her childhood dreams returns. She is captured and sucked out to sea, then rushed in as the wave gains momentum. She cannot breathe. The surf has the weight and power of all the oceans behind it. It is angry. It tosses her up into the air then crashes her back down on the jagged rocks. She smashes into pieces like a coconut falling on to hardened lava and her insides splash thick, white milk on to the black volcanic rock. The next wave carries her remains back out to sea. No one notices the wave or her death. People mill about on the beach as if nothing has happened.

After the nightmare, she pulls on a loose shirt and jeans and rises to get a drink. The dawn is beginning to urge its weight across the shuttered windows. Cowrie is unimpressed. She gulps down her half shell of water and steps from the porch to the backyard. Purposefully, she heads for the fish pond. Peni's net rests against the scraggy kiawe tree. She flicks it from the branch and tucks it under her arm. At the pond, Cowrie places the net on its side in the water, jaws wide and facing out. She then dangles her left foot in the wet space directly in front of the net. The pond remains still. She can see dark shapes at the shaded end but cannot make out individual fish.

Impatient, she reaches into her hip pocket and takes her Joyce Chen fish-gutting knife from its polished wooden sheath. She cuts a small gash across the soft flesh on the inside of her thumb, wipes the blade across her shirt and places it on the rock beside her. She dangles her bloody thumb in the water just in front of the net. There is a sudden ripple from the far end of the pool. Like fire sizzling up a lit fuse, fish rocket swiftly through the water, fighting to be first to the blood. By now, half a dozen fish are struggling in the mesh, turning on each other in frenzy. Blood still oozes from her thumb, but Cowrie will not let go of the net. The fish try to drag it into the murky depths of the pond. With a sudden flick of her wrist, she lurches it from the water and on to the rocks. Two fish escape back down the slithery lava. But one is caught thrashing wildly.

The fish is cut free and spins on to the dry earth. Its tail and then whole body flick from side to side violently. Its gills open and shut with rapid movement. Cowrie remembers the nightmare. The water surging through her lungs as she is dragged back through the ocean and then flung high and dry, gasping for breath. It is time to act. She picks up the knife and launches it into the gills. With a swift flick, she beheads the struggling beast so that it cannot sink its teeth into her flesh. The head lands in the dust by the bushes. One of the mangy cats ventures out for a feast. The eyes are still moving. They seem to follow her as the cat mauls into the bones and flesh.

She turns the remainder of the fish on to its back and kneels astride the body. With her knife, she makes a clean incision in the soft, light flesh between the gills and runs her blade down its belly. The tip of her blade hits a hard backbone, but the gut is soft and bloody. The knife stops short of the tail and Cowrie reaches her hand inside to rip out its entrails. Blood oozes down her arm and on to her shirt as she tears out the guts and flings them towards the bushes. The rest of the cats pounce on to the wriggling mound to devour it.

The flesh is tough and grey inside, like stingray. Cowrie slashes it into chunks, hearing the backbone break as each slice falls off. The remaining fish in the pond are strangely silent. The sun cuts its way through the dawn and stabs into her rounded back as she bends over the fish. The stench is hideous. This is no ordinary ika. When she has finished, she throws the rest of the meat to the cats. That should last them a while, she thinks, running the knife between a folded banana palm leaf to clean its blade. Then she wipes it across her jean thigh for good measure, places it back in its shiny wooden sheath and moves to the side of the house.

The bloody deed over, Cowrie strips off her clothes and stands under the makeshift shower – a hose coming out from the house and suspended over the branch of a tree. She lets the already-warm water trickle down her face and then gush through the valley between her breasts and out over her wide and beautiful belly. It has formed itself into tiny rivulets by the time it reaches her thighs and drips down between her legs and over her calves. She sobs tears of bitter pain that has accumulated over years of having to confront prejudice.

Cowrie is surprised that she could act so violently. Normally, gutting a fish isn't a big deal, but this one was a sacrifice. It was utu. She felt driven to complete it. At least it has been in private and brought the repressed pain and tears to the surface. She has been waiting a decade to let this out and now it is done. Her body begins to relax. She washes her clothes under the hose and hangs them on a branch. In this heat, they'll be dry by the time she leaves.

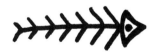

Dear Suzy — what shall I do? You're my oldest mate and I need to talk to you. I think I've just committed rape. Or murder. That's what it feels like. I attracted a fish into my net with the bait of blood and then I kneeled astride its wriggling body and gutted and beheaded it alive, then slashed it savagely into chunks and threw it to the shrieking wildcats. Yes, me, the non-violent protester, who sailed to Muroroa to protest nuclear testing. Can you believe it? It was no ordinary ika. No ordinary act. I did it deliberately and I wanted it to hurt.

Why? Well, there's a het woman here I'm attracted to. All she did was raise that bullshit about how every woman needs a man and I went troppo. She's very intelligent and strong but also traditional. She's only been apart from her hubby for a short time and hasn't yet questioned heterosexist assumptions. But it was enough to heat my blood into boiling lava-sizzling, hot rage! The pond fish here are like piranha. They'd already attacked one of Koana's kids. I'd been thinking of netting one. But when it happened, I was so shocked at the way I exacted revenge.

As you know, I've always been against violence in any way, shape or form. So what does this mean? Could I ever rape or murder? Or was I symbolically refusing to remain a victim? No one knows I did it. There's no way I'd hurt Koana or the kids. But what's the difference? How can people butcher animals daily and not be affected by this? Or do you end up doing it so often you get numb to the feelings?

Don't worry – I'm not about to go on the rampage – but as a shrink – let me know what you think. Please pass on my love to Marewa, Sandi, Penny and all the others at Rape Crisis. You can drop me a line c/- Koana at Na'alehu P.O., Hawai'i. You always said to write if in need. Well, I need you now, Suzy.
Thanks, dear friend.

Cowrie.

The journey up the coast from Puako to Waikui then across the northern tip of the island to Honoka'a is quiet. Nele sits next to her, while Koana has a turn in the tray with Peni. Cowrie is relieved that she will not have to make small talk with Koana and is delighting in Nele pointing out the sights. Koana was withdrawn at breakfast. But thoughtful. Cowrie relaxes enough to let go of her pain and knows that Koana will either talk about it when she is ready or distance herself and never refer to it again. That's usually the way it goes. In the meantime, she does not want her forced revelation to spoil the trip for the twins or for Koana. She knows they have picked up on some tension because they are much quieter than usual and go to great lengths to try to please the adults.

Nele points to a dilapidated church. It is surrounded by palm trees and looks incongruous out there in the fields. Cowrie is surprised at how like Tai Tokerau this farmland is. Gently rolling grassland, greener than she'd expected for the heat, and dotted with familiar cabbage-tree groves.

Honoka'a lies ahead and from there, according to the map, it is a straight run down the coast to Hilo, where they will stop for lunch with Koana's aunty Meleana. Cowrie is already planning how she can get out of it. She has let go some pain, but she still needs space. She will drop them off and shelter under a beach palm to have some quiet time alone. But she must find a way to do this without offending them. Maybe Koana will be glad not to have the dyke friend from New Zealand with her. Who knows?

Cowrie decides to concentrate on enjoying the coast drive. They travel roads high above the sea nudging vertical cliffs that dive perilously into the crashing surf below. The vegetation is lush. Mist hangs in the valleys and through it, scarlet lehua blossoms brighten up the dense shades of the pounamu slopes. It's as if some huge hand issued out from the heavens and sprinkled red stars over the green tree tops. Cowrie recalls odd lines from New Zealand poetry, where the bright red pohutukawa blossom becomes a symbol for the blood-shed on the beaches, the rite of passage as a new breed of colonial breaks through the crusty exterior of the British colonels and farmers who first took the land from its original inhabitants. Captain Cook was finally eaten on a beach in Tahiti. Cowrie bet the pohutukawa were in full blossom that day.

Recent lava trails cut a black river through the valleys amongst which small trees and new growth battle to replace the flow of Pele's fiery anger. From Pape'ekeo, it is an exhilarating drive on roads cut into the vertical cliffs which reveal surprises at each bend. The cream and yellow insides of the wild ginger flowers, ooze their sap on to the grass below, while fiery orange bird-of-paradise spikes thrust out inviting purple tongues. Startling yellow stamens erupt from the sticky interiors of stark white lilies that lap up the bright sun. Water bursts over the edges of bulging cliffs sending spray twenty-feet out from the rocky ledges and thundering into pools below. The sweet smell of frangipani hangs in the wind as they sail past and the landscape explodes with erotic energy. By the time they reach Hilo, Cowrie's desire is satiated and she is beginning to feel human again.

Hilo is very different from Kona. Older and more run down. Yet it has a certain charm. Some of the buildings are reminiscent of Hollywood western sets, with large verandahs that hang out over the streets. It is easy to imagine local cowboys tying up their horses to the shopfronts. Cowrie stops the truck and Koana climbs into the cab to direct her to her aunty's house. Koana is careful to have Nele remain between them. She had wanted to get out to join her brother in the tray, no doubt to impress her cousins when they arrived, but Koana tells her to move along the seat and she'll climb in beside her. Cowrie glances into the rear-vision mirror. Peni looks pleased to lord it over the open back of the truck.

They meander through back streets and turn into a narrow road with old settlers' cottages patched up with corrugated iron and canvas awnings. Chickens and dogs wander about the volcanic rock pathways, apparently oblivious to traffic. Koana points to a run-down cottage with large overhangs and scattered garden sheds made from bits of pink corrugated iron. Outside, the porch is framed by cabbage trees and giant tree-ferns grow either side. A dog that looks like a pig lunges towards the truck and Cowrie swerves to avoid it. "Fucken hell!" she exclaims. Koana glares at her for swearing in front of Nele. The dog races towards the truck again and jumps up on the back as they grind to a halt in the driveway. It splashes licks all over Peni and, behind it, a large woman with handsomely greying hair and an armful of purple hibiscus flowers ambles up to greet them.

"Aloha, Meleana," says Koana, stepping out of the cab to hug her aunt.

"Tutu Meleana. Tutu Meleana," cries Nele and slides down into her arms.

Cowrie glances behind to check that Peni has escaped from the licking embrace of Cerberus. A tall, handsome Hawai'ian man is lifting him off the tray. Must be Mr Meleana, she thinks. Sure enough, he comes around to the front and embraces Koana. His name is Hale. Then a much older man limps over. The twins obviously adore him and they hang on his every word. Cowrie is about to excuse herself and graciously back Honu out of the drive, when the old man comes up and opens the cab door.

"So you're the wahine from our far islands, eh? Koana's told us much about you. She said you were strong and beautiful. And so you are." He laughs wildly, admiring her ample body.

Koana looks shy. Cowrie is amused.

Koana introduces the New Zealander to her relatives and they gather round and ask questions about the "little Hawai'i of the South Seas." Cowrie can hardly refuse them. They make her feel so welcome and, after all, this connecting is why she came in the first place. She follows them into the house and is overwhelmed with nostalgia. Everywhere are pictures of family members – grandparents, parents, aunties, cousins, sons and daughters, in frames draped with flower lei. Cowrie is surrounded by beaming, laughing faces. Round faces on large bodies. Like hers. She can sense them move with the laughter. Suddenly she feels absurdly happy. The events of the past twenty-four hours move into a more distant place in her emotions and she is pleased to banish them. She knows they will resurface the next time she is honest about herself. But for now, she is content to relax with the voices, music and laughter.

A feast has been cooked for their arrival. There is roast pork and boiled kalo, dishes wrapped in leaves, steamed potatoes and carrots and, of course, plenty of poi. The dinner is superb and Koana's family treat her as whanau. They ask many questions and seem genuinely interested. Like Mere's family, they are great talkers and great listeners at once. Before dinner, they give thanks to Pele, bless the meal and afterwards sit around on mats under the shelter of the overhang to talk and sing.

The old man, who Koana introduced as Ika'aka, has taken a particular fancy to Cowrie and shows her his room. All his furniture is outside under a roof of corrugated iron, with his bed in the corner. He insists it is the best room in the house. A butter-churn sits next to his bed to hold the old tobacco tins and papers. Hand-carved furniture takes its place alongside old beer crates. Broken coconut shells litter the floor. It is like a museum of one man's life. Turns out his wife died a few years ago and the family took him back in when the '76 lava flow destroyed his house. They knew it was coming, borrowed a truck and managed to rescue most of the furniture.

Cowrie finds Meleana's father intriguing. Perhaps Apelahama was like this? He was as tall, in the photos, and as handsome. Was he an old character or a tyrant? Why did he desert Hawai'i for a few miserable extra dollars in New Zealand? Did he ever have family here before meeting her grandmother? Were they in love or did he do the best with what he had in the new country?

She points to a 'ukulele hanging from one of the kiawe trunks that support the roofing iron. A turtle is etched on its shiny wooden belly. She asks about the instrument. Ika'aka says it was made by one of the masters – a real craftsman, Apelahama.

Cowrie is astounded. "That's my grandfather," she utters.

" 'Ae, I know," he replies.

"How do you know?" Cowrie asks, and wants to demand why he didn't tell her earlier that he knew her grandfather.

"Everyone knew him. He was one of our best musicians. His fingers were made by the gods. They could fly over the frets." He takes the 'ukulele down and demonstrates the rapid movement.

"Will you tell me about him?" asks Cowrie, humbled by his awe for her grandfather.

"One day," replies the old man. "The time is not right yet."

This is all Cowrie needs. She has scrimped and saved with years of fruitpicking and scratched, torn hands in between her studies to make it over to her grandfather's homeland to find out more about him, her family's past. Finally she discovers someone who knew him apart from

Keo and now he says to wait a while. Stuffed if I'm going to play the detective forever, thinks Cowrie.

"So when will the time be right?"

"You will know," he replies.

"How will I know?" she pleads.

"You will know," he answers, looking out over the heads of his family and up towards the far slopes of Kilauea. Cowrie follows his eyes. She hopes that the right time doesn't involve another brush with Pele. She decides to behave herself in the meantime, just in case.

Koana's family convince them to stay the night. There is plenty of room in the open air under the pink corrugated iron awnings.

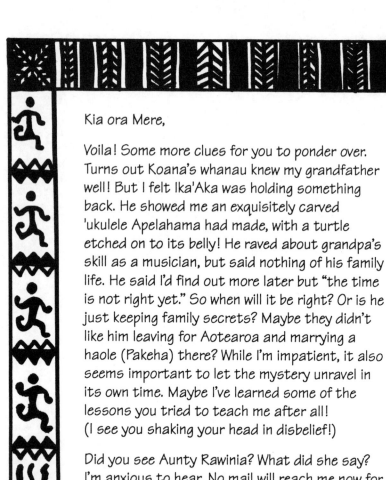

Kia ora Mere,

Voila! Some more clues for you to ponder over. Turns out Koana's whanau knew my grandfather well! But I felt Ika'Aka was holding something back. He showed me an exquisitely carved 'ukulele Apelahama had made, with a turtle etched on to its belly! He raved about grandpa's skill as a musician, but said nothing of his family life. He said I'd find out more later but "the time is not right yet." So when will it be right? Or is he just keeping family secrets? Maybe they didn't like him leaving for Aotearoa and marrying a haole (Pakeha) there? While I'm impatient, it also seems important to let the mystery unravel in its own time. Maybe I've learned some of the lessons you tried to teach me after all!
(I see you shaking your head in disbelief!)

Did you see Aunty Rawinia? What did she say? I'm anxious to hear. No mail will reach me now for about a week until we return to Na'alehu. Koana is here and we're taking the twins to visit their cousins then home via the volcanoes. The presence of Pele is everywhere on this island, but especially around the volcanoes. I get a shiver of anticipation just thinking about being in her

crater – like a journey to the centre of the earth. Maybe that's what I came here to discover. The power of the land.

Knowing about Apelahama personally seems less important now. He left enough tokens in his box to bring me to his island. I feel his whakapapa everywhere. You used to encourage me to try to see the patterns of my dreams. They are all of creativity and destruction: the curved bowl of the crater as it embraces and engulfs me, the concave shape of the wave as it sends me towards shore, but also has the power to destroy my landing, like the floating coconuts that get smashed on to the rocks, their sweet milk oozing like blood into the swirling surf. Will the destructive forces cancel out the creativity?

Meeting Koana's whanau reminded me of home. I miss you deeply. If you are in a lot of pain, hold my cowrie shell in the palm of your hand and I will be with you. Talk to me and I'll whisper back through the shell. I love you.

Cowrie.

After a breakfast of kalo and coconut cooked in banana leaves, Meleana gives them a kete of food for the next part of their journey. Now Honu and her crew are sailing their waka down the eastern road from Hilo, heading for Kaniahiku village where Nele and Peni will see their cousins again. Their Aunty Ela married a haole from Texas and Koana is not that fond of him. But she loves visiting Ela and knows that Chad will be at work.

Their arrival is subdued after the excitement at Hilo. Ela is quiet and withdrawn. Cowrie senses that she is not happy and offers to take all the kids down to the village to allow Ela and Koana some time together. She is relieved to see them relaxed on her return. Ela then agrees to look after all the children. Koana tells Cowrie she'd like to take her to one of her special childhood places. Since Hilo, Koana has softened and does not seem to be holding Cowrie so much at arm's length.

They drive down Pahoiki Road towards the ocean. It is the only time they have been alone since Puako, when Koana first seemed distant. Cowrie keeps to safe topics of conversation. Koana appears to be quite open and unconcerned.

Koana advises her to park on the lava near the ocean. She picks up the kete and leads Cowrie along a trail beside the sea, hardly noticeable from the bay. They follow the black rocks and dazzling water until the track leads inland. Cowrie is longing for a swim but Koana cautions her to be patient. She takes a deep breath and relaxes into her surroundings. Huge palms resembling nikau stretch above forming an archway protecting the track. The roar of the sea recedes into the background as they move further into the trees. Cowrie notices one that has the shiny dark green leaves of avocado but it bears no fruit. It is nevertheless lush and inviting.

They enter a clearing surrounded by the largest palms Cowrie has ever seen. Their branches nearly join over a round, deep pond that is so clean she can see every shape and texture of the coloured stones beneath the water as if lit up by moonlight. Black lava-rock, earthen-red stones from the volcano, the white pumice found around the beaches, lie nestled together, glistening in their rain-soaked haven. There is no wind. The silence encircling them, broken only by the faint song of the ocean they have left behind, feels hushed, even sacred.

Koana kneels at the lip of the pond, beckoning Cowrie to join her. She offers a karakia to the water. Cowrie remains silent, breathing in the warm air as the prayer is uttered. Then Koana stands, flicks off her lavalava and dives into the pool. She beckons Cowrie to join her. Shy, Cowrie moves to the shallow end, drops her cloth and wades in slowly. She is amazed to find the water is slightly warmer than body temperature and very soothing.

Koana is like a dolphin in water. Cowrie has not seen her so active and graceful since the hula dance at Keo's when she brushed so warmly against her thigh. She dismisses the memory as soon as it occurs and focuses on enjoying the present. Koana engages her in dolphin play and Cowrie abandons herself to the joy of their reunion. This gift of taking her to a special childhood place must be Koana's way of saying she still cares, that Cowrie is important to her.

Koana is first out of the water and she gestures Cowrie to come up the bank and lie face up on her lavalava. She panics for a moment, then relaxes when she sees Koana taking her lomilomi lotions and oils from her kete and placing them delicately beside the lavalava spread out on the warm earth. She lies down and Koana kneels at her hair, chanting, her fingertips embracing Cowrie's head down to her ears. Then Koana circles her three times and moves to her feet, repeating the ritual. Cowrie tries to relax and forget that it is Koana bending over her naked body. She lets the hands massage her feet and move along her calves, up towards her tingling thighs. When she feels she can bear it no longer, Koana, as if tuned to her spirit, begins again at her head and massages down her body.

Cowrie has never felt like this before. Koana does not just use her hands and fingertips but her entire forearm rolls over Cowrie's body and her elbows delve deep. Koana rolls her over and begins work on her back, discovering an egg-shaped lump hidden under her right shoulder blade. She homes in on it, pushing the energy outwards, releasing the tension. The feeling is painful and delicious at once.

By the time Koana finishes the massage, Cowrie is asleep. Seeing this, Koana bends over her friend, smiling, and kisses her gently on the cheek. She then covers her with the lavalava and settles beside her, deep in thought.

Ever since Puako, Koana has been wondering what led Cowrie to love other women as much as her own 'ohana. She tries to imagine what it would be like to be sexually intimate with any of her women friends. What would Meleana or Aka think of her then? She remembers falling in love with her closest friend, Wanaka, at school. They did everything together. They even touched each other's bodies with intense anticipation and joy every week when their parents met on pepe hahau nights when she and Wanaka were tucked up together in the bed on the open porch. They'd count the stars and make animal shapes with their fingers raised up between the oil lamp and the wall. Then they'd run their hands and fingers over each other's bodies, pretending to massage like their mothers did, but softly, gently. She remembers the excitement of feeling Wanaka's growing breasts beneath her fingers and the way her own nipples would rise and harden to

Wanaka's touch. But they were just children. It meant nothing, surely? It was just a part of discovering their sexuality, a part of growing up.

Cowrie stirs beside her. Her eyes open and she smiles. Koana feels the re-awakened memory of Wanaka stir in her. She looks away. But not before Cowrie has noticed. Koana slips down into the pool. Cowrie watches her swim under water. She slides down the bank and is there to meet Koana when she surfaces. Koana appears shy. Cowrie lifts a wet finger to her cheek and says, "Mahalo, Koana. For the lomilomi magic. Mahalo." Koana glances down into the water then raises her eyes. She bends over and kisses Cowrie on her cheek. Cowrie lifts her lips up to Koana's mouth, but she has disappeared into the water.

Cowrie decides to bide her time. For the remainder of the afternoon, they play in the water and rest close together on the bank, enjoying the warmth. The sun begins to lower and Koana suggests they return. Cowrie agrees, but wants one last swim. She enters the water and lies on her back floating with her arms and legs outstretched like a starfish. Her large body allows her to float effortlessly and this has always been Cowrie's most relaxed way to meditate. Because her ears are under water, she can tune out the earthly noise and tune into the eerie, other-worldly sounds beneath the surface. She dreams of a peaceful existence, hopes that this new layer of richness in her relationship with Koana will not alter the balance and happiness of their whanau life with Nele and Peni and their extended family.

As she floats Cowrie feels a ripple of water beneath her, a fin moving along her back. It has the touch of Koana's fingertips when she applied her lomilomi magic to Cowrie's body. She rolls over and looks down into the crystal-clear water. Nothing but rounded stones, the colours of Pele's crater. She dives to pluck a smooth, red oval stone from the pool floor and surfaces with it. Climbing the bank, she presents it to Koana, who smiles and places it delicately in the waist fold of her lavalava, against the soft flesh of her belly. Hand in hand, they return, following the track through the waving palms towards the sea.

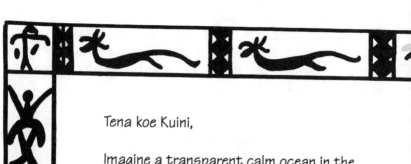

Tena koe Kuini,

Imagine a transparent calm ocean in the midst of that nikau grove we love so much at Karioi, with a base of ochre, cream and lava black stones. Imagine floating on the surface like a turtle, looking down into the centre of the earth with all her sensuality bared naked to the sky. Koana took me to such a place today – her secret childhood retreat. It was like making love. She nearly kissed me on the lips but instead gave me a sensuous massage, her way of expressing her feelings for me. I no longer wanted more. I felt totally satisfied by what she was able to give instead of needing her to be as I wanted her. A few days ago, all my hidden rage at having to repress my feelings as an outsider in my own land, my own body, surfaced and I took utu by sacrificing a hideous flesh-eating fish. Now I feel relief. A letting go. It's as if I can finally accept what is, instead of always wanting what is not. A new freedom for me.

I may come home for the writers' hui and the opening of the new marae.

I love it here but am missing you all and this journey is urging me to get beyond feeling silenced. I'm beginning to think I might have a few things to say! How's your own writing? I loved that story about the eel coming back to life inside the belly of a politician! Haunted me for ages. Take care of your precious self, Kuini.

Arohanui

Cowrie.

They drive down the coast to Opihikao and back towards Kaniahiku on the Kamai'i Road. Koana points out the the ravages of the 1955 lava flow to their left and later, the Pawai Crater and explains that each lava-flow covers a new village, burying history that now remains solely with the inhabitants and talkstory. Cowrie is lured by the power of Pele to alter the landscape as she moves through land sculpted by the hands of a woman who holds within her grasp the power to create and destroy life at her whim.

When they return, Chad is there. He greets them in his Texan drawl, sucks back another swig of Budweiser and burps, hardly lifting his eyes from the Laker's game bellowing out from the huge, colour television which swamps their small living room. Ela looks sad. The children are outside playing in their tree hut.

Cowrie cannot bear to see this woman so downcast. She suggests they go to the village for dinner. Her treat.

"What? In the middle of a Laker's game?" Chad replies.

"Then you won't mind staying here while I take Ela, Koana and the kids to dinner, so long as we bring you some food back," states Cowrie.

"The wife can make me some food first, then you can go."

Cowrie wants to rip out her fish knife and offer him freshly cut meatballs for his tea but thinks the better of it. She knows the dangers of intervening in settled domestic routines.

"No. I think we should let you concentrate on the game.

We'll be back soon with food," she offers, much to the shock of Ela and the amusement of Koana.

"Just don't bring me any of that nigger food wrapped in banana leaves," he yells. "A double burger with fries and a large coke will do."

"Sure thing, pardner," drawls Cowrie, hustling the others into Honu before Chad has a chance to change his mind.

Ela is amazed at her brashness, that she gets away with being so assertive with Chad. Cowrie explains that she's had plenty of practice working with women at the halfway house back home, learning negotiation skills so they can avoid a bashing until they can find more permanent safe housing to live in. "The secret," she explains, "is to let them think they are getting what they want, while getting what you want also. Sane men will want to contribute to a relationship. Only bullies and those into power need to lord it over others. You let them think they have the upper hand until you can escape. Chad's uppermost desire was to watch the Lakers. Second came food. We gave him both and the option of being alone to watch the game. Touché, for now."

Koana asks how long it has been like this.

Ela sighs. She tells them that she became pregnant to Chad at sixteen when he was over in Honolulu on site at a new hotel they were building. He came into the bar where she worked every night. Gradually, they got to know each other. When she found out she was pregnant, he said they must go back to Texas. They went, for three years, but Ela hated it. Then Chad was offered work back in Hawai'i for good pay building a new hotel complex, so he said they could return, for a while anyway. Ela decided that when the work was over, she would not go back to Texas with Chad. She wanted her children to grow up in their native land. But she was too afraid to tell Chad in case he hit her. He had done so before when angry and full of booze.

Koana urges Ela to ask for the support of their extended family and suggests a family meeting negotiated by Meleana and Hale. Chad could decide what to do then and Ela and the kids could stay with Koana or Meleana until it was sorted out. Koana knows that Chad will go back to Texas and hopes it will allow Ela to regain some of her old confidence and begin again.

Koana and Ela work out the dates and logistics of this meeting and by the time they reach the village restaurant Ela's face glows with new hope. The kids are jumping up and down in the tray and Cowrie needs to park before one of them falls off. She pulls up under a tree and its towering arms remind her of lying in the pool, looking up through the palms to the sky beyond, the turtle fin rippling the water beneath her and the feel of Koana's hands on her body. She longs to touch Koana.

Instead, she concentrates her erotic desire on the baskets of food that keep appearing at the other tables in the restaurant. They order a banquet of seafood. The children enjoy sampling but Ela's kids declare they like burgers better than 'ahi. Ela tells them to get used to it because they will be here for the rest of their schooling. That meets with their approval since, apart from burgers and walkmans, they prefer Hawai'i to Texas, where some of the other children bullied them at school, calling them 'coconuts'.

After their meal, they collect the junk food for Chad and head home. He is asleep on the couch, the tv still blaring and a dozen empties littered around him encircling an ashtray of butts. Cowrie waves the food over his nostrils. He is out to it. She leaves the greasy mound beside him.

Koana and Ela share the double bed while Cowrie slings her hammock between the porch posts. The twins sleep in the tree-hut with their cousins.

Chad has left for work by the time they wake. Cowrie packs Honu for the final part of their journey home while Koana and Ela clean the living room mess up. In the night,

Chad rolled over and squashed the burgers flat, knocked over the coke and sent the chips sprawling across the floor. He told Ela never to let that kiwi broad back in the house and he'd get breakfast at work where they knew how to serve a decent meal. Ela wished Pele would engulf him in her lava flow and sizzle up a Double Texan Special: Quarter Pounder plus!

They stay for a strong pot of Kona coffee. Koana makes Ela promise she will call Meleana at the first opportunity and set up a meeting. Then they exchange their farewells before setting off for Na'alehu.

Instead of returning to the main road, Koana suggests they go the coast way, so they drive along Pahoiki Road, past the bay where Koana massaged Cowrie by the pond. Cowrie steals a glance over Nele's head to Koana. She smiles back, her seductive eyes glistening.

Dear Suzy,

Hope my letter didn't worry you too much. I've worked most of it through now. But you always said to share it, let it out, and finally I did. Thanks for listening. No need to reply unless you want to. On the road now with Koana and the kids.

Tell the collective I've finally met the original Neanderthal Man. He's a Pakeha Texan, built like an ox and belongs in Jurassic Park. Treats his gorgeous Hawai'ian partner like she's a slave-mother and he prefers McDonalds to local kai which he calls 'nigger food'! Such a caricature that no one would believe a description of him. I'll leave it to your imagination! Oh, yeah, he's called Chad. That should help! Hopefully he'll return to Texas and Ela will fall in love with a delicious woman like Koana (safe cos they're rellies!) She deserves better, whatever her final choices are.

Thanks for always accepting me, no matter what, Suzy. You, Kuini and Mere are the most constant people in my life. I appreciate that.

Mahalo – Cowrie.

Keo calls Hale and then Ela to find out where Koana is. Ela explains they left about an hour ago and the trip shouldn't have taken more than a couple of hours. That they intended having lunch at Volcano and taking the twins through the Thurston lava tube. No more than three hours in all. But it's been four since they left.

Keo ponders how best to break the news. Early this morning he was woken by a call from the main Ka'u police station enquiring about Koana's whereabouts. He said he could locate her but what was the trouble? The cop handed the phone over to Keo's old mate, Mika, who brought the news and was still at the station.

Mika told Keo he'd gotten up at 4 a.m. to go fishing. When he arrived at Ka Lae, he lowered his rope ladder to the canoe still in the dark. Climbing down, he noticed a large shape bulging out of the cliff. He shone his torch sideways and it fell on Vile's face strangled in the ropes of his ladder, eyes bulging in shock. Mika couldn't get over how frightened he looked. Vile had scaled these cliffs a hundred times and never slipped. Something was wrong.

Still clinging to his own ladder, Mika tried to reach his mate. He couldn't. He climbed to the top of the cliff and drove home to call the police. When they arrived with searchlights, they found Vile's canoe smashed on the rocks below and Aka lying among the wreckage, his neck twisted and the same look of shock on his face.

After the police abseiled down the cliff and dragged both bodies back up, they found machine gun bullets through Vile's heart and lungs and Aka's head. They had been shot from behind as Vile attempted to scale the cliff and Aka to secure the canoe. They reckoned Aka had been shot first and Vile next. Vile had turned to see who fired the shots and the rope twisted around his neck.

Like Prometheus, he'd hung from the cliff, awaiting the vultures. But the birds of prey here were people who owned machine guns and a boat large enough to fire from standing position while its captain negotiated the lethal surf. Perhaps they had wanted it to look like an accident since they had fired at the cliff-face, possibly to frighten the men into falling to the rocks below, then they'd had to finish it off. Or perhaps they intended to warn other fishermen to keep away from their patch.

As he listened to Mika, Keo remembered Vile's tale of their defiance of the US military in rebuilding the sacred heiau on Kaho'olawe. He hoped they didn't go back there and get followed to Ka Lae.

Mika explained Vile and Aka had been away on a fishing expedition for over a week. They wanted to get enough fish to sell around the coast as they travelled and some to bring home to smoke. Mika knew they would never poach the nets of others. Besides, none of the local Hawai'ians had access to such powerful guns or the boat needed to fire them from. It had to be outsiders. But why they had been so violent eluded the police and Mika.

Mika's voice trailed away as the policeman re-entered the room. He took the phone away from Mika and told Keo to contact Koana, Aka's next-of-kin, but not to mention the bullet shots yet. It might stop the police following some leads they had. It was best to say it was just an accident for now. Keo agreed to do this and added he hoped that the police found the bastards. The cops said they'd do their best and put down the phone.

Keo could not go back to bed so he walked into the kitchen and made a pot of kona. He felt sick at the thought of telling Nele and Peni that their father had been shot by some greedy fishermen. But it didn't make sense. All they had to do was warn the men. Vile and Aka were both reasonable guys. And there were still fishing grounds unexploited. They could have gone anywhere.

A deep suspicion hung over Keo all morning. Later, when he told Paneke that the men had slipped in the dark securing their canoe and had fallen to their deaths, she wept. Afterwards, she questioned him more closely. She could not believe that such an experienced fisherman as Vile could put them in such danger. No, it wasn't possible. Keo couldn't say more, but he did add that it seemed strange to him also. Privately, he had his own suspicions. But he'd keep them to himself until he knew.

After calling Meleana and Ela and finding that Koana was due home soon, he excused himself from work at the sugar-cane factory, explaining he had to break the news of the 'accident' to Koana. His boss told him to take the rest of the day off. Keo drove down to Na'alehu and informed the post office that Koana would not be back at work the next day and that Aka had been killed in a fishing accident.

Keo sits on the steps of Koana's house going over the morning's events. The facts, as he knows them, do not add up. But he must not alarm Koana. The news of the death will shock her enough. Even though she and Aka parted ways a few years ago, they were still close and shared the kids well. Peni and Nele were devoted to him.

Keo stares at a pig crossing the road at the end of town and notices a truck outside the shop. Koana getting supplies. He draws in a deep breath and stands, ready for their arrival. Moments later, Honu turns into the drive and Cowrie honks the horn loudly. Peni and Nele are excited to see Keo at their house on a weekday. But Koana feels a lump in her throat. She fears something has happened to Paneke. Or Aka. The happiness she's shared with Cowrie disappears down a steam vent in an instant. The pit of her stomach is on fire, her throat dry. Keo's body is set in rigid stone but his eyes are moist.

Cowrie notices that Keo is not relaxed. He seems to be bracing himself against a strong wind. Koana stiffens beside her. Keo tells them all to come inside. He embraces Koana and holds her for a long time. Cowrie busies herself by lighting the stove and boiling up the kettle.

Keo speaks first. He tells Koana, Nele and Peni to sit down at the table. Cowrie asks if he wants her to go. Keo says no. It is important she hears this too. He explains that Aka has died in a fishing accident, that Vile is also dead. They do not yet know all the details but he will tell them as soon as he finds out more. That the police have been informed. That Meleana and Hale, Paneke and Koana's sister on Maui have all been notified and they will help Koana with preparations for the ho'olewa, along with relatives from Kauai.

Koana weeps bitterly. She cannot believe they have died fishing. She asks endless questions. Keo can only soothe her. Peni and Nele do not understand fully where Aka is. They sense the grief but still expect him to walk in the door. After a while, Koana sends them down the road to Aunty Lukia's. They are reluctant to go but relieved that their mother has stopped crying.

As soon as they depart, Koana breaks out in anger. She wants to know all the details. What really happened. Keo is afraid she will arrive at the same conclusions he has and scream them out to the police, thereby endangering herself if the military really was involved. The cops are hand in hand with the US military and will be sure to protect each other. He assures her that he will tell her as soon as he knows more, that he also feels strange about the accident.

Cowrie feels helpless. She wants to comfort Koana, yet she hardly knew Aka. They only met on that one fishing expedition. She remembers the eerie chill that stiffened her body as they passed the cliffs at Ka Lae on the way to Puako. Maybe she'd had a premonition of things to come? But why? The story Keo has told them does not seem complete. Were there mysterious circumstances surrounding the deaths? She vows to find out. The best she can do now is be here for Koana and the twins.

That night, after Nele and Peni are in bed, Cowrie asks Koana if she'd like to sleep alone or would she like some comfort. Koana wants Cowrie near and spends most of the night crying quietly into her breast. But she is distant again at breakfast, after the kids leave for school. Cowrie suggests she take Koana up to Paneke's. She knows that neither of the women have transport and each will want to be there for the other. Koana nods, and adds that she'd like some time with the children, so perhaps Cowrie could stay at Paneke's for a while.

Cowrie agrees, on the condition that Koana calls if she needs anything. Cowrie senses that Koana is retreating into her grief and it may take a long time for her to come back again. She mentally prepares herself for the weeks ahead and collects her books and a few supplies for Paneke.

Paneke holds Koana, crooning into her cheek. Then she leads her to the lomilomi room out in the open air, surrounded by trees. While Koana is undressing, she shows Cowrie how to light the fire under the steambath. It is an octagonal building made of timber. In each wall is a stained-glass window featuring Hawai'ian myths. Under the building, which is raised on poles, is a clawed porcelain bath, visible from the floor of the steamhouse. Below, an iron cauldron holds the tinder.

Cowrie likes playing with fire. She begins collecting the driftwood and timber from Keo's pile by the side of the barn. She is glad to be of use, able to help Koana in some way. After she has stacked a few cardboard boxes with a pyramid of driftwood and kiawe on them, she lights the end of a rolled taper of the *Hawai'i Herald Tribune* and offers it to the pyre. There is a whooshing noise as the flame eats the oxygen inside the boxes and flares up to reach the waiting driftwood. At that moment, Paneke's ritual chant marks the beginning of the lomilomi treatment. Her cry seems to fuel the flames and a wave of fire engulfs the bath and nearly reaches the floor of the steamhouse. Gradually, it dies down, as does the chanting, until an unearthly silence fills the valley, interrupted only by the passing wingbeat of a manuku.

Her next task is to carry buckets of water into the steamhouse which will be used to douse the flames and encourage the resulting steam to issue up through vents in the floor. A bit like preparing a hangi, thinks Cowrie, having watched the men heat up the stones and later throw water over them to steam the food. Here the stones are across a grate directly above the bath. Both the water in the bath and the heat off the stones contribute to the steam.

She feeds the fire many times before it is hot enough to generate the necessary steam. It is hard work. Sweat pours down her body. Smoke surrounds the bath until all that can be seen are the claws. In the distance, Cowrie sees Paneke and Koana gliding towards her. Koana's face is so serene, so beautiful. Carefully, Paneke guides Koana into the steamhouse and motions Cowrie to join them.

When Paneke opens the door, steam billows out and the three women enter the misty cavern. There are wooden benches at different heights and Paneke takes Koana up to the nearest rung gesturing Cowrie to the next so she can more easily exit to replenish the flames. Koana is now sobbing in Paneke's arms.

The cooler air hits Cowrie's naked body each time she leaves the steamhouse to add logs to the fire. They have been inside a long time. Paneke gestures to her to let the steam gradually die down. She smiles and invites Cowrie up beside them, on the other side of Koana. Koana looks at her through a haze of steam and lays her head on Cowrie's shoulder. Now able to move, Paneke whispers to Cowrie that she will make some herbal tea and to bring Koana in when she is ready. Cowrie nods.

Paneke disappears in a cloud of steam and Cowrie settles comfortably beside Koana. Their shoulders lean against each other and the glass beads run down their bodies until it is impossible to tell whose sweat is dripping on to the floor. Cowrie holds the stone weight of Koana's grief. Her eyes are glazed and her breath slow. Her rounded body glistens with moisture, shines a copper-gold glow into the wooden cave. Cowrie cannot bear to look at her for too long. Instead, she begins to make out the shapes and colours of the stained glass.

As the steam thins, the window facing them slowly emerges revealing Pele on her fiery path down to the ocean to meet her brother whom she has turned into a shark. Her flaming hair trails down her back and over the slopes of Kilauea, sparking into sizzling waves as it hits the ocean. A shark waits beneath the water.

She cannot see the next window but the third one is closer and the steam thinner. Gradually, a woman emerges through the mist, riding the surf, her hair trailing in the sea. A wave circles over her head and she looks frightened and elated to be surging through the ocean. Cowrie squints. Steam obscures her vision. When it rises, she makes out a small head in front of the woman. She is riding a sea turtle.

This revelation excites Cowrie. Is this the turtle depicted on Apelahama's coconut shell fragment, or Ika'Aka's 'ukulele? In the bowl Keo handed her at their first meal together? On the rocks at Puako? Is this the woman in Cowrie's early nightmares?

Koana's body goes limp. It is time to get her out of the steamhouse. She leans on Cowrie who gradually eases her down the ledges and over to the door. The cool air stuns them. On Paneke's guidance, Cowrie places Koana carefully on the bed, brushes her dry with a towel then lays a duvet over her. Koana looks so peaceful. She is only partially conscious of the movement around her. Cowrie bends and kisses her gently on the forehead and Koana manages a faint smile.

Out in the kitchen Paneke is preparing food. She sends Cowrie outside to pick ti-leaves to cook the pork in and to dig a few potatoes and kalo. With the meal steaming on the cooker, they sit down to fresh green ginger tea. Paneke slips Diane Aki into the tape deck and turns the volume low so they do not wake Koana. Cowrie smiles, as memories of their day together in Pele's crater swim across her emotions.

"So you've grown fond of Koana, eh?"

Cowrie nearly splutters tea across the table. "Yeah. She's a good woman. And I like Nele and Peni a lot too."

"So I see. Does that mean you'll be around for a while?"

Cowrie is surprised at Paneke's directness. Does she know about her feelings for Koana or is this an acknowledgement of their friendship? She replies that she wants to remain with Koana and her children as long as they wish her to do so. But Koana needs some time alone with them and has asked if Cowrie can stay with her and Keo until Nele and Peni come to terms with Aka's death.

"That's fine," answers Paneke, and tells Cowrie that she is 'ohana to them and can stay as long as she likes. That it's good for Koana to have a break to deal with this loss on her own terms. That the lomilomi and steambath will reach the deepest part of her grief and the way from here is up hill.

Cowrie asks about the funeral process and how she can be of help.

Paneke replies she can be her assistant in preparing the food and that the ho'olewa will take place in Ka'u with several days of weeping, talking and feasting afterwards when all the relatives will gather. Aka's family will then take the body back to Kauai to be buried where he was born.

"The loss is great, but the gods will look after him," explains Paneke.

Cowrie wants to ask if she believes that Aka and Vile died in an accident or whether there is more to it but she senses the time is not right. Perhaps an enquiry after the funeral will yield further details. She remembers meeting Vile and his tale of the rebuilding of the heiau on Kaho'olawe. She wonders if the US military who shot at them that night finally tracked Vile down and Aka happened to be in the firing line also. She has a fair idea that Keo suspects this and perhaps even Koana.

Paneke turns over the Diane Aki tape. This is Cowrie's favourite song, where she sweeps into mystical high notes from the guttural earthy ones. Paneke swings in tune with the music as she minds her pots.

"Paneke, remember when I asked you and Keo about the woman riding the turtle on the coconut bowl that first night we met . . . "

"Laukiamanuikahiki?"

"Yes. Can you tell me more about her?"

"What do you want to know?"

"Well, she fascinates me. She seems to surface wherever I go. And you have her depicted on that round stained-glass window in your steamhouse."

"She is a powerful figure for us too," explains Paneke. "The stories vary from island to island, but this is what I know. A visiting chief, Maki'ioeoe impregnated Hina and left her with a child named Lau-kia-manu-i-kahiki. That means, 'Leaf for a bird trapping in kahiki.' He asks that she send the child to him in a red canoe with guardians clothed in scarlet robes. In Kuihelani, he plants a beautiful garden of palms and sculpts a bathing pool in the middle. When she discovers the truth of her origin, she refuses to travel by canoe to Kuihelani. So two grandmothers, who know she must go, roast bananas and cause a bamboo shoot to sprout carrying the child high into the skies until she is lowered down again in the chief's garden. There she becomes close friends with a beautiful girl and they make lei in the garden planted for her and bathe in its sacred pool, where a turtle comes and rubs her back . . ."

At this moment, Koana walks dreamily into the room. Her dark hair flows down her back and her lavalava is tucked around her waist. She kisses Paneke then Cowrie and thanks them for taking care of her. She takes the red stone Cowrie dived for in the pool and shows it to Paneke, placing it gently on the table. Cowrie, still stunned by Paneke's retelling of the story of Laukiamanuikahiki, and remembering her day with Koana at the sacred pool, tries to utter, but her lips do not move.

The joint funeral for Vile and Aka is held over the next few days and their bodies taken by their families to their respective burial sites. Koana misses Cowrie but is glad to have some time with her children to prepare them for life without Aka. Cowrie sees her daily but returns home to Paneke's at night. Koana is immersed in memories of her marriage and what it means to have her former partner no longer here.

Cowrie realises she must create another focus, which normally her work would provide, so that she does not centre all her emotions around Koana. She reads Paneke's books on healing and the ancient art of lomilomi and uses her writing as an outlet for her feelings. Paneke is fascinated by her sketches of the rock drawings at Puako and explains many of the symbols to her. She talks with Paneke about Apelahama and comes to realise that her journey has wider than personal implications, that she has a role to play in claiming her ancestry along with all the other mixed-blood Pacific people, and in deciding what responsibilities lie with this knowledge. Paneke is sure this is why Apelahama guided her back home to Hawai'i.

Every night Cowrie dreams of Koana. As time passes, she becomes more afraid that Koana will distance herself further, finding the struggle to assert this new kind of friendship too difficult in her circumstances. The old nightmare returns. But each time, in mid-flight, she swims back into the wave. She never lets herself be smashed upon the beach. Mere has taught her how she can perform such miracles in her thoughts. Gradually, another dimension creeps in. She swims back out to sea yet the other turtles do not recognise her. The experience has altered her. She is alone.

One morning, she wakes up in a fevered sweat, her lavalava on the floor beside her. It is hot outside, but inside feels like an oven. Then she remembers. She is in a long line of men and women and they are all naked. They have inverted triangles tattooed on to their shoulders and are headed for a concrete building in the distance. As they move inside, they smell the stench of burning flesh. The men grasp each other. The women hug one another. There are tears. The heat is unbearable and the stink of gas rises to engulf them.

Cowrie can bear it no longer. She has to get up. She walks out to the lomilomi space and sits on the edge of the platform gazing into the heavens. She feels dwarfed by the sky. From up there, her presence would be like watching a person walk through the Kilauea crater from the rim. A black ant making its way across a hot lava field. What chance does it stand? The odds are stacked.

She takes in a deep breath. She can not, will not give in to this feeling. After all, she did manage to prevent herself from crashing on to the rocks by diving back through the wave in her dream. Surely she can apply this to her fears now?

Clouds obscure the moon. Some relief. The night rains are about to descend. Cowrie hears the downpour in the distance as it comes over the mountains from the west coast. She drops her lavalava, walks on to the grass and stands naked with her arms outstretched, waiting for the wet relief the heavens offer her. Rain descends, first in gentle drops then in large translucent sheets. She surrenders to the power of the water and it feeds her with renewed energy.

The next morning, she sleeps in. Paneke brings her some pineapple juice and tells her that the sugar cane workers say the giant sea turtles are back at Punalu'u Beach. She suggests Cowrie visit them and drop her off at Pahala on the way so she can get to Hilo for a meeting. Cowrie offers to drive her all the way but Paneke says no. She enjoys the bus ride, meets friends she hasn't seen for a while and likes the driver. Cowrie laughs, agreeing to take her to Pahala.

"Good. Then you can swim with the turtles," adds Paneke as she leaves the room smiling.

Cowrie grins. There is a touch of Hinekaro in Paneke. She knows how to get her way while pleasing others. Grabbing a T-shirt, she hitches her lavalava around her waist and joins Paneke at the table. She ladles fruit into the coconut half shell which they always leave out for her. As she drains the last drops of juice, turtle woman looks up at her. There is no fear in her eyes. She rides the wave with jubilant power.

"Paneke, did you finish telling me the story about the child without knowledge of her origin whose real father asked her to be sent to him in a red canoe? Koana came in at the part where she and her girlfriend bathe in the sacred pool and a turtle rubs her back . . ."

"Laukiamanuikahiki. Well, I stopped at the nice part. When she arrives, she is not recognised at first and an oven is ordered to be built for her death."

"An oven?" For a moment Cowrie freezes. She remembers her nightmare. "Surely an oven is a terrible fate for a supposed mistaken identity, especially when the grand-mothers landed her in the chief's garden without her consent?"

"There's no arguing with chiefs, Cowrie. Life was different then. But don't worry. She never ends up in that oven. An owl sweeps over. It is really her aunt who assumes the form of an owl and she chants out her name and lineage and displays the tokens of her birth. The chief recognises her as his daughter."

"What tokens? I don't remember you mentioning them before."

"When the chief got Hina with child, he left a feather cape, a bracelet and a whaletooth necklace so he would know it was really her when she returned."

Cowrie thinks of the offerings in Apelahama's box which led her to Koana, and through her, Keo and Paneke. She has a lot to be grateful for. She secretly wonders what might have happened if the two girlfriends making lei in the garden by the sacred pool had run away together. What the touch of the turtle has to do with her.

"Thank you for telling me the tale of Laukiamanui-kahiki, Paneke."

"Ah, I see you can actually say her full name now, eh?" grins Paneke.

"Yeah. I've been practising."

"So, you ready to go?"

"Sure. I'll just get my togs and fire up Honu."

"Togs? What's a tog?"

Now it is Cowrie's turn to laugh. She races back to her room and returns with some bright purple, shimmering material. Holding it up, she says, "Some people call them bathing costumes. We call them togs."

Paneke is amazed. "Where does that word come from?" she asks.

"Who knows?" replies Cowrie. "Somewhere hidden deep in our colonial heritage, no doubt."

Amused, Paneke repeats the word over several times.

Cowrie knows that by this time tomorrow, half of the Hilo shopkeepers will be muttering the mantra togs . . . togs . . . togs.

Kia ora Mere

We returned home to find Koana's former
partner, Aka, and his friend Vile dead.
(Vile was the fisherman who told me how
they rebuilt the sacred heiau on the island
captured by the US military.) I – and I think
Keo – suspect that the military took
revenge. But no one is willing to state it out
loud. It's not like the boys at Waiouru
playing war games on the slopes of
Ruapehu. This is for real.

Koana is in shock. Paneke gave her a
lomilomi treatment and I learned how to
make the fire for the steambath beneath
the steamhouse.

Then Paneke told me more about the turtle
woman myth: how an aunt turned into an
owl and saved turtle woman from the ovens
by chanting out her lineage and displaying
the tokens of her birth. Suddenly, it all
came together for me. Apelahama left
those symbols in the old box for me to

discover my heritage, rescue myself from
oblivion, find a strength from my whakapapa
to face the future.

There's another side to this. I dreamed I was
in a line of gays at Auschwitz, walking into
the gas ovens. I couldn't stop it happening in
my dream. But now I feel a new power. The
aunt turned into an owl and saved turtle
woman from the ovens. So can we be crafty
and clever. We need to be, to survive.

What do you think? You can tell me in person.
I feel I am ready to return to Aotearoa now.
Last night I dreamed you were calling me.
I heard your voice through the boiling mud of
Whakarewarewa. I hope you're ok. I want to
come home for the opening of the new marae
and for Kuini's writers' hui also. And to take
care of you as you took care of me.

I love you, Mother.

Arohanui,

Cowrie.

Paneke clears her post box at Pahala on the way. There is a letter for Cowrie from Mere. Sent to Na'alehu post office c/- Koana and posted on. Mere seldom writes unless it is important. She prefers face-to-face contact. Cowrie rips open the letter while Paneke exclaims over the telephone account increase.

Mere wants her to return home for the opening of the new marae. They need someone to help co-ordinate an arts festival to coincide with the opening and Cowrie's name was put forward at one of the meetings. Mere feels it is her responsibility to accept, that she has been called to work for her community, that she should be honoured. Cowrie is relieved. She feared that Mere's letter might contain bad news of her health. At the bottom of the page is a PTO. Cowrie turns the paper over and sees all her patterns for the tukutuku panels laid out across the page. They remind her of some of the markings etched into the pahoehoe lava flows at Puako. In the far corner, Mere has scrawled a note: "Rawinia's herbs worked better than expected. Ka pai. Tena koe, Cowrie."

Suddenly, she is brimming with desire to see Mere again, relieved that she is all right.

"What will you do?" asks Paneke.

"I want to return home and yet a part of me wants to stay here also. I must talk to Koana first. Maybe she and the twins will be able to come and visit me in Aotearoa sometime. If I go home, I can raise some money for their airfare."

"Mere is missing you, Cowrie. Your community needs

you there. We can look after Koana. She will miss you too, but I know she will understand. You must trust me on this."

"Mahalo, Paneke. You are right. It will be hard for me to tear myself away from Koana and the twins, but perhaps the time is right to do so now. I can return later when . . ."

Before Cowrie can finish, she bursts into tears. Paneke holds her close against her chest.

"There, there, Cowrie. You can swim back into the wave. There are many more opportunities to come."

"But I love Koana, deeply."

"I know, Cowrie. I have known all along. Your face, your whole being is aflame when Koana appears before you. Like Pele's fire lighting the slopes of Kilauea at night. I don't have to be a magician to see this."

Cowrie is shocked her feelings have been so transparent. "So you don't mind?"

"How can caring and loving of this depth be wrong? You have given the gift of yourself to Koana, Nele and Peni. That is the greatest love you can offer, Cowrie. Never forget this."

Cowrie is overwhelmed with relief. She thanks Paneke. Just in time. She notices the old bus drawing near in the rear-vision mirror. As it crawls to a halt in front of the post office, she helps Paneke out of the truck.

"Go and see Koana now. Discuss this with her," urges Paneke, as she boards the bus. Cowrie promises she will.

Watching Paneke depart amidst the rattle and dust, Cowrie feels torn apart. She knows she wants to go home, back to Aotearoa. Back to where she was born. Yet a strong part of her now feels she belongs here at Punalu'u, Pahala, Na'alehu, on the Big Island, Hawai'i, her ancestral home. She feels split at the root.

Koana looks pleased to see Cowrie. She invites her in for some kona.

"I've got some news to tell you, Koana," begins Cowrie.

"Not before I've explained some things to you," replies Koana. "I know you've been hurting, holding yourself back, wondering why I allowed you to get so close then held you away . . . well, I want to explain as best I can."

Cowrie is surprised. Koana seldom opens up like this. "It's ok, Koana. I know you need time to get over Aka's death and . . . "

"Kulikuli, Cowrie, kulikuli!"

Cowrie knows this is a warning to be quiet and let Koana continue. She'd heard Paneke use it.

"You know that Apelahama and my grandmother, Kini, were friends?"

Cowrie nods.

"Well, I found out from Ika'Aka that they were more than friends. Tutu Kini was betrothed to Pakile, whom I knew as my kuku, grandfather. But my mother, the first born daughter, was thought to be the daughter of Kini and Apelahama. When your grandfather left for New Zealand, Tutu Kini and Pakile married immediately but according to Ika and others, she mourned the loss of Apelahama for years afterward."

Cowrie is stunned. "But why didn't you tell me this before?"

"Cowrie, listen to me. You know that day when I gave you lomilomi and then we kissed, or nearly kissed in the pool?"

How could I ever forget it, thinks Cowrie.

"A part of me wanted to respond to you. Even though I do not understand how two women can survive as lovers, I enjoyed being close to you. At that moment I wanted to kiss you. To be intimate."

"So what stopped you?"

"Apelahama. Don't you see, Cowrie? You and I are blood relatives, 'ohana. We share the same grandfather. It would be kapu. It is forbidden."

Cowrie is excited for a minute, realising that her instinct is not wrong, that Koana did feel the intimacy by the pool. "But Koana. We don't know that for sure. Besides, isn't that out-dated now? I mean – we'd be kapu anyway because we are two women."

"No Cowrie. You don't see. This is important to my family, therefore it is important to me. I cannot betray their trust in me."

"Or maybe that's a good protection against the un-known?" Cowrie offers, feeling selfish to be pushing at the borders when Koana is being so giving.

"Paha. But even if it were not so, I could never be sure that it would be what I'd want forever. I must think of Peni and Nele as well as other family members."

"But surely Nele and Peni would love it? They adore us being together."

"Yes. But would they feel the same when they are older, when the school kids start teasing them and the local community isolates them for having a mum who is kapu?"

Cowrie thinks back to the roasting her friends' kids got on Waiheke Island, where the lesbian mothers became a big issue at the local school. Another small island. Everyone knows everyone's business. Different attitudes divide into opposing camps and fester underground rather than being aired openly. Koana is right. Here, it'd be centuries of tradition to fight. And it would be Koana who would have to bear the brunt of the prejudice, not her. It becomes more complex when large extended families are involved and different cultural expectations preside. On the other hand, friends like Paneke might understand.

"You're right, Koana. It would be a big move and it would have to be considered carefully. Besides, you don't need to worry. I've decided to return home anyway."

"Not because of me, I hope."

"No. I've just received news from Mere. She wants me to come back for the opening of the new marae and the local community suggested I co-ordinate an arts festival to help celebrate the occasion. I need to do this, Koana. It is important to me. But I feel split. I don't want to leave you and the twins."

Koana is relieved that the subject has changed and that she has actually had the courage to face up to Cowrie. She promised Paneke that she would explain about Apelahama and warned the others not to say anything until she was ready to share the news. She had to know she could trust Cowrie. It was important to keep Tutu Kini's honour – even though a few people suspected her mother was actually Apelahama's daughter. Had it not been for her feelings for Cowrie, she would have kept the secret forever.

" 'Ohana. Whanau. So you do understand a little of what it is like for me here then, Cowrie?"

"Yes," Cowrie mumbles, thinking of Mere and her lifetime of devotion to the child she found at the Rawene Orphanage. "But I do think some people may be more understanding than you think, despite the old ways. They will recognise love for what it is, in all its forms."

"What makes you so sure, Cowrie?"

"Just a conversation I had with Paneke. I think she might understand."

"Yes. Paneke might. But the others are not all like her. And I need time to sort out my feelings for Aka. What this means for the twins and me. Where we go from here."

"Yes. I recognise that. Just know you are always welcome to visit me, us, in Aotearoa, Koana. I'll miss you.

I wish we could have been lovers . . . "

Koana puts her finger to Cowrie's lips. She takes her hand and guides her to the lomilomi table. She delicately strips Cowrie and places her face down on the towel. Then she begins the ritual call. Cowrie is in the crater. Pele is calling her from Hale ma'uma'u. She rises up from the steam vent and flies over the crater surface. Below her, boiling mud and lava. Steam obscures her vision, then thins. Mere's face appears, singing her name. Mere is pulling something out of the boiling mud. She cannot make out what it is. Then she is swimming. Her feet are being sculpted so that they are webbed and can help her carve her way back out into the waves. Her arms are shaped into fins . . .

Cowrie wakes to feel Koana's fingertips moving from her breasts up to her neck and face. Her body is liquid to the touch, flows with the movement of Koana's fingers. She has no idea how she came to be on her back, but is so relaxed she does not care. Koana massages the lines of her face with the touch of a lover and bends down to breathe hot air on her cheek, her ear, as if to seal the sculpted shape her hands are creating. Cowrie's eyes remain closed, hoping this will never end, when she hears a faint whisper in her ear "Laukiamanuikahiki". She drifts back into a deep sleep.

Cowrie rises late the next morning. A half papaya is left for her breakfast, so she squeezes lime juice over it, licking her fingers and reaching for the phone to book her flight home. Then she drives down to Punalu'u and makes for her favourite part of the beach between the coconut-fringed lagoon and the jade-green sea. Closing her eyes, she imagines what it will be like to be home, to see Mere's face again, share all she has learned, get her perspective on things, hear the local gossip. She can't wait to begin planning for the festival. Maybe Kuini will help organise a writers' hui with her.

Local kids run past her, kicking up sand in their wake. They plunge into the water and swim out fast. There is splashing, then calm. One of them is riding a sea turtle, his hand gripping the shell just behind the turtle's neck. The others scream in delight. Each of them wants a ride. The turtle seems unperturbed. Cowrie stands for a better look. Behind them, more turtles appear.

As if called, she enters the ocean. A lone turtle is up her end of the beach. Cowrie lies floating, waiting to see if it comes near. The turtle approaches tentatively. Cowrie can see its eyes just below surface level. The turtle suddenly swims under her, emerging at her feet. Cowrie turns and it dives again. The turtle is playing with her. She dives beneath its belly. Its eyes follow her, swivelling around like a tuatara. Ancient eyes. Knowing eyes.

By now, they have drifted out beyond the breakers. Realising this, Cowrie starts a strong breast-stroke inland. The turtle swims alongside. She sees an incoming wave and strikes out to catch it. She pounds the water with her strong arms, lashing and kicking her fins to create a backwash behind her. The wave lifts her up and she lunges into its concave belly. The turtle is right beside her, coasting in on its crest. She thrusts her fins outward for balance. The water draws her under as it gathers momentum to power her to shore. Cowrie holds her breath until she thinks she will burst. Then she surfaces, skimming across the glassy waters at the edge of the black sand. The turtle is no longer with her.

Cowrie struggles to stand in the swirling water as the wave slurps outwards. She searches the sea, scans the horizon. Nothing. Scrambling up the beach, she sees a nob out beyond the breakers. It floats and dips in the swell, hanging in the balance, waiting. Then it disappears beneath the surface.

Further up the beach, at Punalu'u museum, visitors stream in from the buses. The guide begins telling them about the 1868 tsunami. Cowrie walks towards the museum. She decides she should see it before leaving. She is elated. At least she can tell Mere the turtle really does swim back out through the wave. She touches her coconut shell carving, knowing she will return to Hawai'i and enters the museum just in time to hear the guide explain about the twenty-foot wave that swept over Punalu'u beach in 1975, destroying everything except Kane's mural which depicts the beach and heiau as it might have been two centuries ago.

Cowrie looks past him to the rounded mural. At the far end of the beach Kane'ele'ele rises up out of the sea spray like a vision. It is exactly as it was in her dream. She can hear the laughter, smell the sea air, taste the poi being pounded in the bowls on the sand. A coconut is split open. She rolls its sweet milk on the tip of her tongue, lets it drift down her throat. An old man stands in the middle of the beach waving a fan of fresh leaves in welcome as he guides a waka safely through the breakers.

"But how could a tidal wave splash up the walls and miss this mural?" a tourist asks.

The guide shakes his head, as if expecting the question. "Punalu'u is protected," is all he says. He remembers his grandmother telling him how a turtle's head was seen at the tip of the tsunami, how it guided the wave in and then swam back out and watched over the beach protectively before diving deep and disappearing from sight.

Cowrie smiles to herself and walks out on to the hot lava sand. She glances back towards Pele steaming up out of Kilauea and follows her hair-line to the foot of the mountain where she meets the crashing ocean. She faces south towards Ka Lae. Next week, she will sail her waka back to Aotearoa. The black sand of Punalu'u will still be visible between her toes when she arrives. And in her body, a new power, a new knowledge about survival. A connection with her creativity that no one can crush.

At the end of the beach, she imagines Kane'ele'ele rising up out of the stones, canoes moored in the lagoon behind her. A waka leaves from the shore, bound for a distant land in the far south seas. A land no one has dared yet imagine. A land of incomparable beauty. Islands that are connected to these beneath the water. Islands that draw their spirit from the same family of gods. Land of the awakening dawn. Aotearoa.